BALCONY
OF
FOG

RICH SHAPERO

BALCONY OF FOG

A NOVEL

HALF MOON BAY, CALIFORNIA

TooFar Media
500 Stone Pine Road, Box 3169
Half Moon Bay, CA 94019

Library of Congress Cataloging-in-Publication Data is available.

ISBN: 978-1-7335259-2-3

Cover artwork and design by Adde Russell
Artwork copyright © 2020
Additional graphics: Sky Shapero

23 22 21 20   1 2 3 4 5

Also by Rich Shapero

Rin, Tongue and Dorner

Arms from the Sea

The Hope We Seek

Too Far

Wild Animus

1

Through a ceiling of fog, the storm flashed, blanching the night and the drenched forest. The men in the narrow canyon looked up. Each wore a head bulb strapped to his brow. One of the bulbs was shorting. Arden joggled the bulb, but it wouldn't stop blinking. The rain slashed, the wind hooked him and rasped in his ears, while the invisible thunderhead rumbled, brewing a fresh charge.

His face felt raw, and his arms were prickling—he might have been sick with a fever. He could feel the electric field in his blood and his bones. "Put it down," he shouted to another toiler. Neely, tall and thin, was working a long metal pry bar between the loose sections of a sluice. They were there to repair the breakage. The torrent ate at the canyon's right bank, threatening to overtop it.

"Go," Arden yelled, motioning the toilers forward. Together they threw their weight against the uncoupled section, trying to move it back into place. Each wore a harness with a twin cable attached—one to prevent them from being washed down the sluice, the other to power the bulbs on their heads. Their effort moved the broken sections closer together, but not close enough. The torrent crashed past, disappearing over a steep drop-off eighty feet beyond.

"Use the bar." Jiggers, the foreman, stood on the left bank, snarling. "Neely—"

Arden swore and wiped the mud from his face. Neely looked at him, and Arden shook his head. Beneath his leather leggings and sheepskin slicker, he could feel the electric pins in his flesh. His brawny body quivered. His large hands buzzed, knuckles glowing.

"Neely—" Jiggers waved him forward.

Neely gripped the pry bar with his bare hands.

"Close the break," Jiggers ordered the gang.

"Fool," Arden muttered. Was it rain or the charge hissing? The air was crackling like fat in a fire.

The men put their weight against the sluice section, while Neely worked the pry bar. Then the section pivoted, and the men recoiled. The flood mounted the right bank and flowed over it.

Jiggers turned his anger on Neely. "The bar, damn you."

Arden ground his jaw, thick and unshaven, eyes deep. Neely, always willing, followed Jiggers' orders and turned to attack the sluice again. Then he stumbled. Struggling to keep his balance, he raised the pry bar over his head.

With a deafening crack, a wire of lightning flashed through the fog, crowning the pry bar with a bursting star. Neely juddered and collapsed, folding into the torrent. The mitered joint of the sluice caught him and ripped through his arm. The water carried him toward the drop-off. Ten feet before, he reached the cable's limit. He bobbed there, hunched and tumbling.

Arden wheeled and descended the canyon, feeding his cable through his wet hands. His head bulb's circuit closed, the beam solid again.

"Get back to the break," Jiggers shouted. "We'll fish him out later."

Arden ignored him. The torrent swirled and foamed through the dark rocks of the drop-off. He could see it curling, plunging down the sheer cliff. He reached Neely, knelt on a boulder and circled the man's chest. Half drowned, Neely stared at the drop-off, arms jerking, the torn one bleeding from elbow to wrist.

A motor roared to life behind Arden. The cable attached to his harness was moving. They were winching him in. He kept his feet beneath him, levering his legs, dragging Neely with him. As the winch drew him closer to the gang, Jiggers yelled at him. "Alright, you're a hero. Now fix that sluice." He pointed at the break. "Both of you."

Neely cradled his lacerated limb.

"Lift him out," Arden said, arm still around him.

"I'm at my limit with you," Jiggers warned.

"He's hurt," Arden said.

Jiggers raised a club and swung it at him, short by a foot.

"Raise him," Arden yelled.

Neely was shaking and jabbering. The other toilers were motionless, watching. One had retrieved the pry bar. Jiggers roared at them all, then he waved his arm at a man standing between him and the rusted control box. "Hoist him up."

The twin cable was raised over the wheel of a derrick, lifting Neely out of the canyon. His head sank with relief. Blood flowed down his forearm and dripped from his fingers. The derrick rotated and released its load. Neely buckled in a heap on the bank.

Jiggers barked at the toiler by the control box. The man pulled on his sap-soled overboots, unclipped Neely and attached himself to the cable. Manning the controls, Jiggers pivoted the derrick, lowering the toiler into the canyon to join the gang. Arden turned back to the break in the sluice.

Without warning, the winch motor roared again, and Arden was jerked off his feet. Jiggers was raising him on his cable, yelling at the gang to finish the work. As they grunted and muscled the sluice section closer to its mate, the derrick swung Arden over the bank.

Jiggers didn't lower him. He watched Arden hanging there, smile ripening as he raised his club. "Coward," Arden said.

Jiggers struck his thighs, then his hip and his chest.

"Rat, slave," Arden gasped. His arms swung, but his fists didn't connect. Jiggers struck his belly. Arden groaned, sucking for air.

"You want this?" Jiggers huffed. "Take as much as you like."

The club squealed as it struck the wet leather over Arden's groin.

Arden curled, knees jerking up, hands raised to his head. Jiggers barked and stepped closer. As he raised his club, Arden yanked the electric lead from his head bulb and jabbed it at Jiggers' neck. The foreman did a dance, eyes blank, mouth wide, his body spasming. Then the circuit broke.

Jiggers drew back, raising his club.

When he powered it around, the blow struck Arden's head.

A toiler can dream. No tyranny on earth will quell hopeful thoughts.

As Arden lay in the mud beside the river, he dreamt he was free. On his back, in the bottom of a boat, gazing up at the stars. Drifting.

When he woke, the storm was still raging above the fog, and the rain was heavy. He was soaked, but his body had been covered with a tarp. In the mud by his hip was a hand weapon, a cat dart. There was a toiler's bandana too, with three hardcakes inside it.

Arden rose to his knees and then stood, seeing the sluice. The sections were mated, channeling runoff into the torrent. The gang was gone, and so was the control rig and derrick. All that remained were the power cables, coiled and snaking over the ground. His head throbbed, and when he put his fingers to his brow, they came away bloody. The bulb was still on his head.

He put the hardcakes in his slicker pocket, gripped the cat dart and scouted the riverbank. Arden took a step. His belly ached, but his legs seemed fine. In the east, a half-moon glowed behind a veil of mist, and the flashing of the thunderhead lit the riverbank's puddled soil. He started along it, shivering with cold.

Downhill was the forest, the trunks of tall trees silhouetted by fog. Uphill, the ziggurat came into view, vivid then dim as the sheet lightning flashed and the rain poured down. From its gleaming mass, power mains descended the slopes like the arms of a centipede, touching outbuildings and winding into the forest. The settlement was on high alert. A bolt had blasted the granary, the brickyard was flooded, and the rows of lit windows were flickering. Even at Apex.

Arden started up the pathway toward the ziggurat. He could see the Colonnade at its summit. At the center of the pillared enclosure, smoke was rising. It coiled through the pillars and above the peaked roof, where the wind caught it and carried it into the sky. Priests were making offerings to the rain god that threatened them.

He cursed and halted. The smell of the smoke sickened him. A fresh stab of pain drove through his head. *Have you had enough?* he thought. Arden turned, peering into the forest. He looked down at the dart in his hand. Its housing was rusty. He touched the dart's head and the coiled spring, wondering if it would fire.

He checked the pathway again, then he headed in the opposite direction, hurrying his steps, entering the woods, finding his way through the swirling mist with the storm flashing over him.

The leaf mold was thick. He stumbled his way between giant trunks, skirting thickets, scouting the way, dart at the ready. The light in the sky strobed on the sword ferns and huckleberry. The rain fell in silver curtains, folded and glittering. He watched for the long, lithe shadow in the scrub, or the glint of eyes in the web of branches above. Knee-deep fog essed before him, hiding the earth. The loam was puddled, and as he moved, he heard the splash of his boots.

Arden paused by a snag. Behind him, nothing but rain and forest; and above, the storm, flashing through the branches. As he watched, the high fog thinned, and the thunderhead appeared. White thorns and wires glinted within, lighting the char-colored boils from beneath. A glowing bolt plunged into the forest, the earth shook, and the *crack* stung his ears. There was no denying the storm's power. It was fearsome to behold. A creature of flesh felt small, slinking beneath it.

The fog thickened, hiding the storm again. Arden skirted a large boulder and halted before a tangle of boughs. He checked the forest around him again, then he put the dart in his pant pocket and began clearing the boughs away. They choked the mouth of a dark ravine, hemmed by firs.

A strange noise stopped him—a deep sucking, like the sound of a flood in a storm drain. The sound grew to a *whoosh*. As Arden straightened himself, the earth seemed to sink beneath him. Rain was no longer falling. The drops were suspended, moving sideways, circling slowly. The *whoosh* continued to mount. The trunks around him quivered and the raindrops expanded, filling the air with glittering bubbles.

What was happening? Was it the wind, the storm? The peculiar sound, the strange sensations— He'd never felt anything like it.

Then, as quickly as it had begun, the *whoosh* faded. The bubbles burst, and the trunks were once again motionless. The storm's rumble returned, along with the showers. Arden gazed through the treetops, trying to pierce the fog. A rain god's magic, he thought. That's what the priests would say. They would spin some foolish story about it—a story that would frighten children and invade their dreams. As much as he despised the beliefs, the fears were still with him. They were part of a past he couldn't erase.

Arden returned to his task, and when the entrance to the ravine was clear, he stepped down into it. On either side of the entrance, spears were ranked. It was like a dark cave, roofed over with branches, sheltered from the rain. He felt his way through the dimness and plugged in his head bulb. Light filled the space, powered by a buried cable he'd spliced in on the sly.

To one side was an oblong shape, thirty feet in length, with blankets draped over it. Arden peeled off his slicker and his soaked shirt. He removed the blankets, and the hull of a boat appeared. Arden shook one of the blankets, shedding needles and bits of lichen and moss. He wadded its corner and used the cloth to polish the name chiseled on the prow: *Mariod*. Then he draped the blanket over his shoulders and set to work.

A mast lay to one side, half covered by duff. He dug out the rudder assembly, placed it in the boat's stern and packed it with moss. Next came the patchwork sails, and with them, the memories of the weeks it took to stitch them together. He secured them in the bows. He paused to inspect a joint on the stern, fingering the heads of the pegs, and then he ran his hand over the hull's waist caring not to pick up splinters. He could feel the boat's desire to be in the water. And he could see where the seams were sealed and the narrow band above the waterline that remained to be caulked. He would finish that once she was afloat. The plan was finally in motion.

Then he turned to the piles of crates filled with stolen supplies and began lifting them into the craft. As he worked, he spoke softly—to the boat, or the spirit within him that longed to escape. Or perhaps he was speaking to the wood from which the hull had been fashioned. The boards had been trees, tough trees, and they still held the memories of all they had endured. Then the words melted into a murmur, a hum, following a melody he'd learned as a child. A song Mariod had taught him about enduring tribulations and keeping hope alive.

His need and his hope, the song from his past and the rumbling and flashing—wove a spell. And out of that spell, a strange presence emerged.

He had shifted the light from his head bulb to the roller logs ranked at the rear, when he stopped, sensing something.

Between the storm's rumblings, he heard a twig crack.

When he turned, a woman was standing at the mouth of the ravine—naked, dripping, lit by flashes, with the fog boiling behind her.

Their eyes met.

She covered her breasts with her arm.

The woman looked desperate. Mistrustful. She was shivering. Her blond locks were drenched and draggled. Arden glanced at the *Mariod*, wishing there was some way to hide it. Then he faced her again and stepped forward.

She stiffened. He halted.

He motioned her toward him.

She didn't move.

"You must be freezing," Arden said.

She didn't reply. With one eye on him, she probed the ravine.

"What are you doing here?" Arden asked.

She took a step, and another, trailing a scarf of fog behind. She faltered, extending her arm, fooled by the uneven ground, as if she was carrying a burden she was unused to. The shadow of a trunk halved her face. She paused, swaying, touching her thigh, grasping her shoulders, regarding herself as if her body was strange to her.

"Come out of the rain," he said.

He closed the distance. She cried out when he picked her up. Then her head tipped and she went soft in his arms.

Arden set her down on the duff beside the *Mariod*. In the light from his head bulb, he saw her face clearly: lips like waves trimmed by the glare; arched brows, a high forehead; and the soft edge of her nose.

He removed the blanket from around his shoulders and covered hers.

"You escaped from the Rink," he guessed.

Before she could answer, the forest was shaken by thunder.

Her eyes flared. She looked behind her, then up at the sky, as if she expected some doom to descend at any moment.

"You're frightened," he said, trying to understand.

Another flash and a nearby *crack*. The wind howled, beating the roof of branches.

"Ingis," she hissed, still looking up.

"The rain god?" Arden laughed.

"How bad is it here? This blanket feels like wool. And the light on your head— You haven't returned to the stone age," she said.

Arden wasn't sure how to respond.

"He didn't want me to leave," she said. "If he finds me, he'll take me back."

"Who?" Arden asked.

"Mad," she said. "Impossible. Fawning, degradation— It was endless. I was no better than a common cumulus to him. Food for his ravenous ego."

She's barely aware I'm here, Arden thought.

"He's going to destroy himself," she said. "That's how it will end."

A flash overhead silvered her hair. She pursed her lips and shuddered.

"You're cold."

She flinched and looked up. The branches above her clacked in the wind.

She's beautiful, Arden thought.

The woman shook her head. "All a dream. A delusion. I never loved him. I never did."

He grasped the blanket. "You have a name?"

"Estra," she answered.

As he closed the blanket around her, Arden noticed a frond-shaped scar, branched like a bolt, embossed on her left breast.

"Ingis did that."

Her eyes were clearer. She's seeing me, he thought.

"I was seduced by his charge. It was— Irresistible. Addictive. I was afraid I couldn't live without it."

She glanced at the boat and the web of branches that formed the cave. Her arms fell. She looked ill.

"'King of Heaven,'" she smirked. "Where am I? What land is this?"

"America. The western coast. You're not from around here."

"Are you listening to me? Do you live here, in the forest?"

Arden shook his head.

"Is there a city nearby? Is that where you're from?"

"A settlement," Arden said. She's from a city herself, he thought. Schooled. Good with words.

"Is it safe in your town? I need a place to stay. Out of sight. I don't know— Maybe he'll give me some distance. For a while—"

"Our settlement isn't a good place for most of us," Arden said.

"Who is it good for?"

"A few at the top."

Estra pulled the blanket around her. "You've been patient with me." She squinted, as if she was trying to see him more clearly. "What shall I call you?"

"Arden," he said.

She noticed the sharpened stakes resting against the fir trunks behind him. Her gaze narrowed and shifted, spotting a pile of torches and clubs, and the spears by the entrance. "You're well armed."

"Not well enough. There are cats in the forest. Crag Cats. They hunt at night."

"Why are you here?"

He regarded her for a long moment. "I'm working on the *Mariod*."

"Your boat."

He nodded. "I don't want anyone to know about it."

"I can keep a secret." Silence filled the space between them. Then the storm cloud resumed its grumbling. "Maybe I could help you."

Arden didn't reply.

"Where do you live?" She cocked her head.

"In the ziggurat. A communal lodge."

"Can I stay here, under your boat?"

"That wouldn't be safe."

"Because of the cats?"

He nodded.

"Is there somewhere else?"

"You could—" He stopped himself.

"What?"

"Stay in my cell."

Her eyes were edged with suspicion. "What does that mean?"

"Nothing. I'd sleep on the floor."

"Can I trust you?" She spoke softly now, gently.

"I'd have to sneak you in."

"Because—"

Arden imagined how his return would be received.

"It's not allowed," he said.

When they reached the edge of the forest, he led the way along a cutbank, holding a blazing torch in one hand and a spear in the other. Arden was bare chested. Estra wore his slicker with the hood pulled over her head and the blanket around her waist. Her pace was slow, her steps cautious.

The trees were dark and dripping, and above the ceiling of fog, the storm still thundered and flashed. The ziggurat appeared at the top of the rise, a stepped pyramid with nine levels. The lines of windows flickered, the power still wavering.

"What were you humming?" Estra asked.

"An old song," he said. "'Hard Trials, Great Tribulations.' Mariod taught it to me."

"Mariod again. A woman you loved?"

"She was my nurse at the Nest," he said, "on Level 7."

He waved the torch at the cutbank, lighting the round mouth of a storm drain.

"This is secret too," he said. "I come and go without being seen."

"Don't worry," she said.

Arden hid the spear in the scrub and stepped into the drain. The flow reached his calves. He could feel Estra's hand on his shoulder.

When he turned, he saw fear in her face. "Move slowly," he said. "Don't stumble. The drain steepens as it climbs the slope." Then he sent his legs forward, sloshing through the flow, holding the torch in one hand, moving the other along the curving wall.

A scream sounded behind them—raw, agonized, rising in pitch, like some beast being flayed. Estra halted. When Arden turned, her face looked chalky. The scream came again, echoing in the drain.

"A cat," Estra guessed, eyes wide.

Arden nodded. "A female."

The grill of the storm drain lifted. Arden doused the torch, hid it in the weeds and rose. He grabbed Estra's arm and helped her out. They were at the border of the brickyard, behind the ziggurat. Thick power mains snaked from the generator bunkers. Arden hurried her beside one, scanning the grounds. The roof of the curing shed was gone. The mill wheel had frozen and the slaughter pens were flooded.

A deafening crash, a blinding strike—

Estra raised her head. "That's him."

The storm cloud was above them, its neck thick and sooty, the roiling crown lit by a brewing charge.

"Hurry." Arden pulled her with him.

As they reached the delivery bay of the commissary, the rear doors of the ziggurat swung open. The low notes of an organ sounded, and a pair of cowled priests appeared. A cortege followed, bearing the burnt remains of the sacrifices toward the holy plot beyond the sheep paddock. The bodies were covered in sacramental cloth, but as the bier moved, a blackened arm joggled loose of the wrappings.

Wind blasted the commissary. The earth shook and a dazzling bolt drove from the storm's livid head. It touched the roof of the livestock barn and the walls exploded. People appeared, shouting and shrieking; animals lurched and raced in every direction, their backs on fire. Arden pulled Estra into the stockroom and through the kitchen.

They entered a corridor lit by flickering sconces, crowded with jostling men. Guards were shouting orders. One led a group toward the explosion, while priests moved among the others, urging calm. The organ was audible, tragic, ponderous, groaning and shrilling in the narrow passage like a wounded mammoth. Arden led Estra through the melee toward the first floor landing.

Her grip was firm. He could feel the tension in her arm and the fear in her stride. He felt fear too—fear of the storm's rage, and fear of discovery. As they approached the landing, Arden spotted Jiggers hurrying toward them. Did the foreman see him? His head turned, but he strode right past.

A group of nurses had gathered on the landing and were leading a prayer beseeching the god. One recognized Arden and smiled. He returned the greeting and led Estra up the stairwell to Level 3. He paused at the top and peered down the corridor, looking for the foot patrol. Nothing. Then they were stepping past the cell doors. A man exited one and started toward them. Arden nodded to him.

"Around the corner," he murmured to Estra.

He halted before a narrow door, turned the latch with his key, entered his cell and drew her inside.

In the darkness, the small bed was visible, his dresser and the chair by the window. Arden hung his head bulb on a hook over the dresser and plugged it into a loose wire. The light flashed on. Estra moved to the window and drew the curtains apart. He came up behind her.

The thunderhead was no longer over the settlement. It was moving toward the forest again, its dark billows churning like a thick stew. All at once, the earth beneath it erupted. A sooty funnel reached down, sucking everything into its vortex. The sky around the storm was crazed with electric webs, the boiling head glowing and furrowed. It was an image from Arden's childhood, a picture in a storybook: the mushroom cloud loosed during the Four-Day War, source of the faith, father of rains that had plagued the people before he was born.

"He thinks I'm in the trees," Estra said. "He's trying to drive me into the open."

Arden searched the billows for human features. He could see what might have been the curve of a brow and the hollow of a temple. "I don't understand—"

"Those burnt bodies—" Estra regarded him. "They were sacrifices to Ingis?"

Arden nodded. "We're taught to fear the gods. When I was a child, I could see their faces."

"You don't believe anything I've told you."

"I believe you're frightened, that something terrible happened to you."

"And Ingis?"

"You can see anything in a cloud."

Estra glanced through the glass. "That's no god." Her voice was edged with malice. "Ingishead has a face, and it's a reflection of the man inside it."

Arden stared at her.

"I was born in America," she said, "in the east. So was Ingis. We dreamed of a life in the sky, and we left the earth together. I was a young woman then." She turned away from the storm. "I was up there with him."

"How did you come down?"

"Would you believe me if I told you?" Estra cocked her head.

Arden didn't reply.

"I swam," she said.

Over her shoulder, he could see the storm crossing the ridge. Arden imagined a man aboard, sullen, grumbling. As rage twisted him, his bolts lit the mountains and his rains flushed the forests.

"It's moving away." He closed the curtains.

"He was venting his spleen, taking it out on your village."

"The priests will say they appeased Ingis with the sacrifices."

She sighed. "If it were only that simple."

Her pain seemed real. What had happened to her?

"If they find me here," Estra said, "what will they do?"

"Put you with the single women."

"And you?"

"I'd go to Soak. You stand in a tank of cold water."

"For how long?"

"It was three days last time."

She looked around, the bare bulb lighting her lips and her cheek. "Just the one room?" The mud brick walls were bare.

"I'm a person of no importance."

"It isn't much, is it," she said.

He stepped across the room. Estra followed. "It's enough for most of them," Arden said.

"But not for you." She lifted her chin.

"No. Not for me." He opened a closet door and handed her a towel.

She wiped her face. Then he handed her a toiler's shirt and pants, and motioned her behind the door. She changed while they spoke.

"What work do you do?"

"I dig culverts and repair sluices. It's always something. The battle with the rain never ends. Whatever we build, it tries to wash away. Without it we'd have no crops, but sometimes it takes those too."

"How long has the settlement been here?"

"It started as a bomb bunker during the Four-Day War. They built the ziggurat at the end of the nuclear winter."

"How many are there?"

"Close to three thousand," he said. "Most of them men like me. Toilers take up the first six floors. Level 7 is the Nest. Level 8 is for single women. Level 9 is Apex, where the priests and overlords live."

"Why are you—"

"At the bottom?" He spoke softly. "My grandmother belonged to a conquered tribe. I was born to toil, and raised in the Nest."

"Bad luck," she said.

Was it pity she felt? Dismay?

Estra stepped from behind the closet door. His clothes fit her poorly. The pants were baggy, and she'd cinched the waist. As she drew close, he realized she was exactly his height. Not an inch shorter, not an inch taller. He was peering into her eyes. They were mirrors, and he could see the reflection of his own affliction and longing. Whatever reserve existed between strangers, for a moment, dissolved.

"What you saw in the forest— It's taken me four years," he said.

"Please, don't worry. I'm not here to betray you."

"I want my freedom."

Did his words touch her? He waited for her to speak, but there was only the quiet of the mud brick cell, the harsh light of the head bulb, the fading sound of thunder and the dwindling rain.

"You're a smart man," Estra said finally.

"I'd like to be smarter."

She spotted his keepsakes on the dresser, and she stepped toward them. Tree cones, pieces of quartz, bark, petrified wood.

Estra picked up a rounded stream pebble.

"I dream of freedom," he said quietly, "and I dream of love."

He could see the suspicion in her eyes.

"Two people," he said, "knowing each other, thinking the same thoughts."

"Is love like that?"

"When you're free, really free," he said, "love makes freedom worth having. Doesn't it?"

"That depends on who you love."

Was she wary of him, or attracted? Arden couldn't tell. Her eye glinted with an animal keenness.

"I don't know what freedom is," he said. "Or love. But I'm going to find out."

"Are you?" She laughed and set the pebble on the dresser.

Her lips were moist, her teeth small and sharp.

"A determined man can do anything," he said.

"Maybe you wished me here."

He raised his hand. Estra saw the caress coming and she

drew away. Arden touched the air a foot from her cheek.

"I'm not like him," he said.

She raised her brows.

"I would honor your spirit," he said.

"Would you."

The bulb's glare edged her hairline, the flare of her lip, the beam of her nose.

She lifted her arm between them. Then she touched his chest and edged closer.

Arden clasped her shoulders and kissed her lips, and as the contact was made, a fresh hurl of rain rapped against the window.

They drew apart, regarding each other. Her lips closed, and the silence stretched out. Then she was leaning toward him again, lips parting. Arden met them with his, and this time the reserve vanished. He was lost in the kiss for what seemed a long time.

Estra's hands fell to her sides as the embrace ended. "I shouldn't be doing this." She turned, her face in shadow, the bare bulb sheening her golden hair. "I'm so thoughtless about the future. Always— Gambling everything on a moment's impulse."

Was it remorse Arden heard, or an invitation? Where was she from? Who was she really?

"Are you glad I fell into your forest?" she said.

His flight to freedom— Could he trust a woman who claimed she'd come from the sky?

"I'm glad." Estra's eyes glistened. "It's not too late for me. For us, Arden. Is it?"

He put his arms around her. "It's just beginning."

This kiss was still deeper.

When it was over, Estra let her breath out slowly. She touched his sternum. "You've made love," she said, "with the singles?" Her fingers toyed with his shirt button.

"Not with the women on Level 8. There's a place down the valley." He looked away. "The Sweat Rink. They cart us there every two weeks. The women wear masks. It's relief, not love."

She shook her head. "We won't think about that."

They were naked, beneath the sheets on the small bed.

Arden paused, sensing her agitation. "Are you with me?"

"Trying to be."

"I've never felt . . . this exposed."

"It's different for me too," Estra said.

"Am I doing something wrong?"

"No. It's just so physical."

Arden didn't know what she meant.

"Hold me," she said.

He put his arms around her, and as they pressed together, her face lost its border. The rays of her iris were sage-colored spokes, and the hub was a fathomless pupil.

"I'll be fine," she whispered. "You won't hurt me."

Arden's limbs loosened. Their chests drew apart, letting the chill air between.

Estra caressed his cheek. "I've spent half my life dreaming of a man like you. And now you're here."

He touched her breast. It was like driftwood, smooth except for the frond-shaped scar, the mark the current had left, branched over her heart.

He'd felt foolish at first, brutish between her perfect thighs. And then, as her ardor rose, he had worried he would disappoint her. He couldn't match her passion, this animal-woman, this creature who said she'd come out of a storm—

Then, as the end approached, she grew caring, tender. It was her fullness of spirit he felt—a joy rooted in kindness and a generous heart. He'd been a beast of burden, covered with hide; and as he drew close to her, his hide had dissolved.

"I'm in love," he said.

Steps sounded in the corridor.

Arden rose on one elbow and faced the door.

He'd forgotten to wedge the shim under his door. He hurried to the entrance and secured it, feeling stupid and careless. Estra was standing, stepping toward him.

They embraced.

"So frightened," she murmured. "Both of us."

"I hate it here. Every man I rub shoulders with, the women in the Rink—" He touched her lips. It was the first time he'd lain with a woman who wasn't wearing a mask. "I still have my hope. And an angel."

"Your dream of freedom," she said. "Tell your angel about that."

Arden weighed her words. "It's dangerous for you to know."

"Are we going to let fear rule us?"

He regarded her for a long moment. Then he stepped to the dresser, retrieved a knife and strode to the wall above the foot of his bed.

Arden inserted the blade between two bricks, waggled it and slid a brick out. He reached his hand into the hole and removed some folded papers.

"There are clans up and down the coast," he said. "No one knows which ones might welcome a stranger."

"People have left here before?"

He nodded. "Two men, eight years ago. They didn't come back. It's anyone's guess what happened—if they found a settlement, if they tried to survive on their own."

He unfolded one of the papers. A hand-drawn map.

"You could start your own colony," she said. "Make your own rules."

"That would be hard. Where the earth isn't poisoned, it belongs to the cats." He put his finger on the map. "There's the ziggurat. I'm going to float the *Mariod* down this river. And launch it here, in this bay." He spread another map. "This is the coastline north."

"How accurate are these?"

25

"I'll find out."

"No villages are marked."

"I'm going to follow the coast, and hope," he said. "I'll put ashore to trap and forage."

"And at night?"

"I'll sleep on the water. I'll live like that for the rest of my life, if I have to. I'm not staying here."

Beneath the maps was a yellowed page. When Estra raised it, she saw a rough sketch of a woman's face.

"Mariod," she guessed.

Arden bowed his head.

"Is she here?" Estra asked. "Is she going with you?"

"No."

Estra noticed script on the drawing's backside.

"Something I wrote," he said, reaching for it.

"Please. Let me read it."

Arden sighed. Estra scanned what he'd written.

"I've never been good with words," he said, "but that night, they poured out of me. She died at Apex."

"'My never-setting sun.' Beautiful thoughts."

"I vowed if I ever found out who condemned her, I'd cut their throats."

The threat startled her. "She was executed?"

"Sacrificed."

Estra was speechless.

"I was supposed to die with her, but she let go of my hand at the last moment." He touched what he'd written and turned the page over, peering at the crudely drawn image.

"Your hand?" Estra muttered.

"An overlord said she was plain. I guess that's true." He slid the drawing beneath the maps. "She wasn't like you."

"Mariod saved your life?"

Arden nodded. "I've never understood why."

"She knew who you are," Estra said softly.

The cell was silent. She took his hand.

"You're a brave man," she said. "You don't care what others think. You want a good life." She turned his hand over and touched his calluses. "And you'll have one.

"When will the boat be ready to launch?" she asked.

"It's ready now. The sails are done. I've got blankets and cloth, rope, hides, canvas and knives. I can rig the mast and finish the caulking when it's in the water."

"How will you get it down to the river?"

"There's a runoff channel. I've cut roller logs."

"I can help you."

Arden stared at her.

"What about food?" she asked.

"I've been pirating from the commissary. I've snuck a few sacks out. I have a friend in the kitchen. Another week or so, and I'll be ready to leave."

Estra clasped his hand with both of hers and peered into his eyes.

"Do you want me to go with you?" she said.

2

On the north side of the meal hall, the seats were vacant and the benches were wet. A curtain of murky water descended from the ducting. The windows behind were spidered with cracks. Men in the food lines moved past the serving counters, while a pair of young girls from the Nest stood by the water dispenser, singing hymns.

Arden watched the soup being ladled into his bowl, feeling the eyes on him. As he raised his tray and moved among the men seated at the plank tables, the eyes followed him. There was space on the bench beside Neely, and he headed toward it. Neely looked up, shifting nervously as Arden set his tray down and lowered himself.

"They know you're here," Neely said, glancing at a guard posted thirty feet away. "You'll get time in Soak."

"I'm expecting that," Arden replied.

"Soak won't be enough for Jiggers." Neely tried to spread lard on a hardcake with one hand. His other arm was bandaged, in a sling.

Arden moved the cake from his tray onto the table.

Beyond the drizzling curtain and cracked windows, the sky was visible, white and blue. On a platform above the kitchen was a pipe organ. Its silver tubes were quiet, and the organist's stool was empty. Arden glanced to the side, put his palm over the cake, and slid it to the edge of the table and into his coat pocket.

When he turned back, he saw an overlord striding toward him, flanked by two guards. The white caftan swirled behind, brushing the seated men's legs. Arden didn't react. The guards wore dirty leathers like himself, with red caps. Both carried eight-foot pikes, and the cables trailed behind them. He could see the boots of one slowing.

Men across the table stopped eating. Their eyes crept, then froze.

Arden stared at his plate. The overlord and the guards halted behind him.

"On your feet," a guard ordered.

Arden was motionless.

"What's the man's name?" the overlord asked the guard. And when he was told, "Don't be difficult, Arden."

Arden exhaled, swung his leg over the bench and stood, facing the lord. He recognized the man's pinched chin and square spectacles. Above his rolled white collar, the lord's long locks were braided and woven into a crown. His front was crossed by purple sashes.

"We hear you have a visitor in your room," the lord said.

Arden didn't respond.

"Is that true?" The lord squinted.

Arden said nothing.

The lord sighed. "We're picking her up right now." He turned to the second guard and nodded. The man raised his pike, pointed its silver tip at Arden and extended it till it touched Arden's side.

The tip crackled and sparked, and Arden's legs folded beneath him. The pike followed, feeding him current. Arden groaned and twitched on the mud brick floor.

"Enough." The lord raised his hand.

The guard raised his pike, breaking the circuit.

Neely watched.

The guard turned. "What do you know?" He moved the pike's tip toward Neely's bad arm.

Neely's mouth sagged. "He's stealin' food."

The second guard fished in Arden's pockets and pulled out the cake.

The lord sucked his cheek. "Give him a little more."

The pike dipped, jolting Arden again.

"Please—" The lord gathered his caftan and stooped. "Don't force a good-natured man to be harsh. You know the rules."

The lord's shortwave buzzed.

He straightened himself, took the burnished box from his hip and placed it to his ear. "Yes? I see." He glanced at Arden. "That makes sense to me. Well then— The matter's at an end. I can get my breakfast."

The lord returned his shortwave to his hip. Then he turned to the guard with the lowered pike. "Stay your power."

As the guard righted his weapon, the lord extended his hand to Arden. "It seems a mistake has been made."

Arden stared at the man's hand.

"Come on now," the lord said.

Arden took his hand, and the lord helped him up.

"Your room is empty," the overlord smiled. He spread his arms to the watching toilers. "Let's eat."

Arden dipped his head, scanning the cutbank as he emerged from the storm drain. The duffel on his back caught on the drain's flange. He freed it and crossed the stream, winding his way through the trees, stopping now and again to peer behind him. He had hoped he would have a week, at least. They needed food. What he had on his back wouldn't last long.

Estra— She'd appeared in the night, like dew on the scrub. He could picture her lips. And her eyes were green. But she was still a stranger to him— He couldn't recall the sound of her voice or bring her face to mind. And the affair with Ingis— He wished she would tell him the real story. Did she even know it herself?

He passed between the two giant firs, and the mouth of the ravine appeared. The branches weren't as he'd left them. "It's me," he said, and began to clear them away. Estra's arm showed through the tangle, moving branches away from inside.

Then the gap was wide enough, and she was in his arms, whole and alive.

"We were seen," he said.

Her eyes met his. "What does that mean?"

"Things have changed. We're not going back." He set down the duffel. "Food. A little. We're rolling *Mariod* to the river."

"Now?"

He nodded. "We have to leave."

He stepped into the ravine, bent, and began removing duff from around the mast.

Estra moved beside him, looking at the roller logs and the shell of the hull.

"Help me with this," he said.

She knelt and dug her hands in, clearing the humus away.

Then Arden froze.

He could hear a rustling, at a distance. He raised his hand to her, and they listened together.

A moment of silence. Then rustling again. Something was moving through the forest. Arden rose and stepped to the mouth of the ravine, looking back the way he had come, trying to see through the wooden web.

A man rose slowly above a hill lined with saplings. Was it Jiggers? A guard appeared, then two more, each with a spear;

33

and a fourth was behind, with a pack of hounds straining at a pull rope.

The leader stopped, and the guards did too. He spoke and motioned to the others.

"I should have known," Arden muttered.

Estra, beside him now, squeezed his arm. The hounds began to bark.

Arden grabbed the duffel and pulled it into the ravine. Then he clambered out, with Estra behind him, and the two dragged branches back into place, trying to cover the entrance.

"Follow me," Arden said.

He skirted a deadfall, hurrying her through waist-high sword ferns, into a grove of giants. The trunks were blackened, scaly and charred. He straddled a fallen one, weathered to cork and dust, and started up a steep incline. The earth reeked of fungus, the scrub was mottled with lichen. When the incline leveled, he paused and looked back.

The hounds and the men were at the foot of the slope, climbing toward them. Estra's chest was heaving. One of the dogs spotted her. A frenzied yapping, and the others joined in.

Above, the slope grew steeper, climbing to a ridge. The surface was rocky. Arden scrambled up a lane of gravel. Estra followed. When they reached a blocky scarp, he boosted her from below. From there, the way was steeper still and more exposed. They hung on to taps and wiry roots emerging from chinks. On an incline of shards, Estra slipped, splitting her pant leg. Blood soaked through the cloth, but they continued up. Jiggers and the hounds found a more gradual route, vanishing to one side and then reappearing higher on the slope.

As Arden and Estra approached the crest of the ridge, Jiggers halted seventy yards below.

Estra sank to her knees. Arden lowered himself beside her. They were slick with sweat.

"Is he giving up?" she wondered.

Jiggers was watching them, while the hounds leaped and barked. Two guards turned back. The other two remained.

Jiggers raised his arms, cupping his hands around his mouth. "Where do you think you're going?" he shouted.

"He can see," Arden gazed at Estra. "We have nothing. No food, no shelter."

"She'll be cold," Jiggers yelled, "and hungry. How long will that last?"

Estra took a breath and straightened herself, about to answer. Arden grasped her shoulder, shaking his head.

"Come down," Jiggers shouted. "They'll send her to Level 8 or the Rink. If you don't, these hounds are going to eat her liver."

Arden exhaled. "The earth would be a better place without people."

"So would the sky," Estra said.

Her hair was tangled. Below the knee, her pant leg was red with blood. Arden raised the cuff, tore a wad of moss from the mat beside him and sponged the wound. Then he used the heel of his hand to wipe a smudge from her brow. "He's right. We'll be hungry and cold. And at night, there's the cats."

35

He felt his pant pocket. The cat dart was there.

Estra sniffed. "Can you smell that?"

Arden frowned. "Smoke." He scanned the forest below. From a shaded hollow, gray clouds were lifting.

"The *Mariod*," he said.

"No—" Estra's face crumpled. She crossed her wrists over her breast.

Arden imagined the brave boat burning. The prow and stern, the keel, the tiller he'd fashioned with so much care. The lone mast, and every carved peg— His dream of escape had ended. So quickly.

"It's my doing." Estra's cheeks were wet. "I'm the cause."

Arden huffed, confounded. Almost a laugh, but he was too pained for that. He turned away from the coiling smoke, gazing at the ranks of wooded slopes and sawtooth ridges. "I'm not going back," he said. "I'd rather die here."

Estra embraced him.

All at once, the hounds were barking again. Jiggers and the dogs were headed toward them, with the two guards right behind.

Arden stood, and Estra rose with him. He grabbed her hand, and they hurried toward the crest.

They had crossed a stream and mounted a snow gully when the scream of a Crag Cat reached them. Arden stopped, scanning the traverse and the forested valley below. The trunks were twisted, as if a giant hand had tried to uproot them. The sky above them was dark, but the horizon was red.

Jiggers, the two guards and the hounds were silhouetted on a spur nearby, moving quickly along it. As Arden watched, they halted. The hounds were still baying. Then, one by one, the baying stopped.

"What are they doing?" Estra wondered.

The men huddled, and a moment later, the three of them started back down the spur with the dogs, descending into the dimness. The cat screamed again.

"Are we on our own?" Estra said.

Arden pulled the cat dart out of his pocket.

"What's that?"

He checked the trigger release. "If we're lucky, it will fire one shot." He put the dart back in his pocket and scanned the ground. "We'll need other weapons." He stooped and picked up a stout bough, gripped its end and struck his palm. "Move at night, sleep during the day. With piles of rocks close by."

"Could we climb a tree?"

Arden shook his head. "They're experts at that." He gazed at the dim traverse ahead of them. The moon wasn't up, but the sky was clear and the stars were bright. He handed the bough to Estra, then he faced the traverse and started forward.

Hours passed. The half-moon rose, and the stars rotated over them. Arden headed west, toward the coast and the sea, as if hope lay in that direction, the plan for his escape still with him. They were descending a rocky incline when Estra spotted the cat.

"I see eyes," she said quietly.

"Where?"

"On the left, moving through the boulders. It's following us."

Arden looked, seeing only rocky silhouettes. Then a long, lithe body appeared, gliding between them. The cat's eyes glittered like embers.

"Keep moving," he muttered. "Not quickly. Our pace should be steady. Think angry thoughts. We're ready to fight. Don't smell like fear."

He pulled the dart from his pocket.

Long minutes passed. They reached the base of the rocky incline and crossed a dry streambed. The cat was still behind them.

Then a second appeared. Arden led the way up a slope of shelving slabs. The second cat descended toward them, circled to the side and climbed a block, peering down at them as they passed. It lowered its head. Its whiskers quivered, and its tail switched. The cat's nostrils flared and drew in their scent.

All at once, the cat at their rear was bounding toward them.

Arden spun and howled. The cat didn't spook.

With twenty feet between them, the cat sprang, foreclaws reaching, jaws agape, breath hissing in his throat.

Arden fired the dart. The cat roared and buckled, tumbling at his feet.

The cat's eyes glittered. It lifted itself. Still alive, still strong— The dart had torn out a piece of its shoulder.

"You're dead," Arden said, raising the empty housing as if he would fire it again.

The cat shied and bounded into the canyon below.

As Arden returned to Estra's side, the second cat vanished.

Exhaustion finally stopped them. They found a steep-sided spur with a curved reef of rock at its center and bald ground around it. After collecting a battery of fist-sized grenades and padding a small space with moss, they settled themselves.

The moon nestled in the night's velvet. Stars pierced the darkness at every angle. To Arden, the sky seemed enormous—boundless, infinite. His own powers—his command over a perilous future—seemed very small.

If the two cats no longer threatened them, others would soon. Assuming they survived the night, the next day would bring the challenge of food, water, refuge from the weather, and the need for tools. They had nothing. Only each other.

"You may have picked the wrong settlement," Arden said. "And the wrong man."

"Don't say that."

Estra looped her arm through his and gazed at the sky.

"If it's a boat we need," she said, "there are a million to choose from."

High above, a fleet of cumulus clouds were drifting past.

"That would be nice."

"You don't believe me," she said.

"I'm not like you."

"Don't be so sure."

He laughed. "You'd take me with you."

She nodded. "I would. We belong to each other now."

Arden gazed at the fleet, teased by the notion that people could live in the sky. When a real escape was at hand, the fantasy had troubled him. Now it pleased him.

"You'd be different," she said. "Your body would change. And your heart and mind."

"I like the idea. I've had enough grief down here."

"We would live for freedom and love," Estra said. "I could make your dream come true."

"What about Ingis?"

"The sky's a big place." There was a dodge in her voice, as if she was trying to persuade herself. "We could find a peaceful corner, out of the way." Her eyes crossed the heavens, scouting its edges. "A place for dreamers."

"That's what we are."

She raised her arm, pointing. "Look." Estra put her temple to his and sighted along her arm.

He could see it, at the sky's border. A small cloud, floating toward them from the south. Its underside was smooth, like the hull of a ship. Streaks rose above it, like naked masts.

"A simple cumulus," Estra said. "Just mist. No running water or electricity. That's all I ever wanted."

Arden put his lips to hers. He could feel her breath and the throb of her pulse. For a moment, it seemed they had left the earth. They were floating together, with the wind blowing through them, in a place of light and wonder.

"Why not," he said. "We're as fragile as clouds. And our fate is to disappear. To be forgotten."

"Forgotten." Estra whispered, as if praying for that.

She looked back at the sky, and he did too. They watched the clouds drift among the stars. Some twisted. Some lobed. Some had scarves that peeled off like leaves from a cabbage. Her gaze returned to the lone cumulus floating at the edge of the sky.

"Can you hear the swells slapping its bow?" she said.

Arden listened. The call of a screech owl reached him, and he imagined it was the ship's creaking bulwarks.

"You're not afraid?" she said.

"I've been afraid all my life."

"And now?"

"I'm only afraid I'm going to lose you."

The silver light of the moon made the cloud look spectral, ghostly. A wind from the west grooved its underside and canted its streaks. As they watched, billows rose from its top, and its front turned toward them, as if a following wind had filled the cloud's sails.

"I want to know how Mariod saved you," Estra said.

He peered into her eyes, seeing regard and a fierce determination. He took a breath and began.

In autumn the rain gods came, and as usual, ritual offerings were scheduled to appease them. That year, the priests were especially fearful. There was a war in heaven, that all could see. The defeated god was one the priests knew and revered. The victor was a stranger, unhonored, unknown.

A sacrifice was planned to exalt the victor. The Choosing, as always, was in secret. Mariod was prized by many she tended, and she taught the canons. Her respect for authority had never been questioned. Arden was twelve and contrary, often in trouble, but he was well-instructed in the rites of worship and understood that being Chosen was an honor bestowed on few.

The ceremony was rushed. It was midnight, the heavens were pouring, and the new storm was on the move. The two of them were hurried to Apex, and from there, they were led up the stair to the roofed Colonnade. With a guard's permission, Mariod stopped midway to straighten Arden's hair. She looked into his eyes, smiled and kissed his cheek. As they continued up, Arden began to cry.

On top, the rain was fierce and the winds battered the assembly. But the priests and overlords were dressed for the occasion; and despite the pressure of time, the rituals were precisely observed.

The mood was solemn and pious. The priests, all women in black robes, stood in a circle, chanting. A half-dozen overlords, men in white caftans, sat on a dais to witness the ritual.

Mariod's clothing was removed by a priest. A litany accompanied each garment. Naked, she was escorted to the

Throne—a font elevated three feet above the terrace and filled with blest water. The priest helped her up. Mariod took her position facing the assembly, ankle-deep in the pool.

Another litany, and a second priest stepped before Arden and began removing his clothing. When he was naked, she led him to his place on the pavers below the Throne. The wind blew stiffly. He began to shiver. When the priest guided his hand to Mariod's, she was shivering too. Once their hands were clasped, the priest returned to her place in the circle.

An overlord led the group in song. Then a priest wearing a golden crown rose from a hatchway and approached the naked pair. She wore boots and thick gloves. She was holding the end of a long black cable that trailed behind her like a giant worm. She halted when she reached the Throne.

The chanting mounted. Tension showed in the watching faces.

Courage was part of being chosen, and Arden knew that he had to be brave. Mariod began to chant along with the priests. He tried to join in, but his voice rasped and warbled. She squeezed his hand, and her message, he knew, was *be strong, be strong.* At the moment of Contact, all their energy would pass to Him and would be one with His.

The priest with the golden crown lifted the black cable and extended it toward Mariod's head.

Another litany, this one spoken by all. Then a spark leapt from the cable. Mariod shook as the current went through her. When the priest drew the cable back, she collapsed in the pool, smoke rising from her body. Arden was still standing.

The chanting ceased.

He was shaking, but not from the charge. Every eye in the assembly was on him. Mariod had let go of his hand.

Winds caught the smoke and drew it through the Colonnade's piers. Arden stood shivering, waiting. The storm thundered above him, and when he looked up, he saw the face of the god for whom Mariod had died.

Had her faith dissolved at the last moment? Had she balked at taking the life of a child she'd raised? Did she go to her grave thinking she'd betrayed the settlement and its gods—for him?

Finally, the priest who had led him to the Throne motioned him toward her. He was placed in quarantine, until they could decide what to do.

Estra was shaking him. Arden rolled over and rubbed his eyes.

"They're opening," she said.

"Opening?" His head was in her lap.

"The Tunnels." She pointed at the heavens.

Arden didn't know what they were or why he'd never noticed them. But as her finger passed over them, the Tunnels appeared. He raised himself.

The darkness was pierced by silver straws, and there were people swimming inside them. In every direction, near and far, humans were ascending or descending the starry night.

"I'm dreaming," he said.

"Believe what you like. It's time to leave." She craned her head. "We'll use that one."

Arden could see the mouth of a straw above them. Its circular entrance was bright and clearly defined. A *whoosh* mounted in his ears. The air below it was whirling with bubbles.

He peered at her. "You're going back."

She nodded. "And you're coming with me. Take off your clothes."

Arden was too stunned to move.

She pursed her lips and unbuttoned his shirt.

Estra was a different creature than the one he'd snuck into his cell. Unexpected, unearthly. He looked up. Inside the Tunnel was a glittering fog, a slow vortex. The *whooshing* grew louder. Was he going to do this?

They were both naked now. Estra clasped his wrist.

"Imagine you're lighter," she said. "Much lighter."

"That's all it takes?"

"That's all."

As he watched, her body shimmered and misted like frosted glass.

"Come on now," she urged him.

Arden shrugged his shoulders, as if he was shedding a heavy burden.

"You feel lighter?" she said.

She's not human, he thought. She'd been pretending. He could see through her.

"Are you feeling lighter?"

"It's not working," he said.

Her lucid eyes softened. She put her lips to his. They were cold and dewy.

Arden's chest tingled. When he looked, his arms had fogged. He could see through his legs.

Estra rose slowly, and he was rising with her.

"Don't worry," she said.

Arden could see the earth below them, the bald spur with its rocky reef, snow-covered peaks, thick forests that rolled to the sea.

Estra's cheeks were translucent now, her brow, her whole face— She was turning to motes—of water or breath. And so was he. His outline remained. He still had his earthly margin. Some vestige of human integrity held him together.

"What's happening?"

"You're graduating," she said, "from solid to vapor."

Above, the bright mouth of the straw grew larger. Its edge was pearled.

He could feel the agitation of his atomized flesh, and the agitation was mounting. He was like water, boiling, turning to steam. He was losing his center, his border, his shape—

"I don't like this," he said.

They had reached the Tunnel's mouth. As they moved inside it, the sparkling fog swirled around them. Estra let go of his hand.

"Swim," she said.

The transformation slowed. His diffuse body quivered and jelled.

Estra reached with her arms and flexed her legs, and she rose like a silver fish. The Tunnel was all around them.

"You're one of us now," she said.

Us, he thought. People rising into the sky. People retreating from it.

He sent his arm into the fog and flexed his trunk, joining the strange migration.

"Angry," she said, "hurt and betrayed. Abused and abandoned."

"Are they all so desperate?"

"Only they know their reasons for leaving. Or the reasons why, defeated by life in the sky, they choose to return. Swim, Arden. Swim."

He took long strokes with his arms, torso gliding, trying to keep up. The fog churned and glittered around him. Below, out of sight, the earth he'd deserted was falling away.

Would he return? Would he ever be a man of flesh again? He struggled to calm himself. Estra looked blissful, a creature from fable, serpentine, graceful, her hair streaming back.

They emerged from the Tunnel, and invisible currents caught them. They were like two floating twigs drifting away from an upwelling spring. A body so light needed little strength to keep it in motion. Above, the sky was crystalline, jeweled with stars. Time passed as it does in a dream.

Then Estra spoke. "There," she said.

Arden could see it ahead—the cloud, their craft, riding the waves.

Cords of vapor trailed down like mooring ropes. Topside, its billows swelled like sails catching the wind. Opaline light shone on the cloud's gunnels, while above its waist, the moon flashed silver on a rounded mount, like a ship's bridge.

Estra pulled through the roiling sea, a sea of wind and vapor. Arden swam behind her. "We're coming aboard," she cried.

As her voice faded, the moorings dissolved, and their intended home rolled toward them on the evening tide. Arden did his best to follow, stroking, finning his legs and flexing his trunk. The cloud rode up a hill, gleaming before them, sapphire gray. Then it sank, crushing a wave, spattering the bows with copper foam.

Estra was closing the distance. He followed, floating and sinking in the hillocks of fog. The cloud's hull was draped with nets of spume. As she reached the waist, Estra grappled the netting. Arden surfaced beside her and clung.

"She's ours," Estra said, and they rose together, climbing the netting hand over hand. When they reached the gunnel, she rolled over it, onto the quilted deck. Arden followed.

He lay huddled there, catching his breath. The deck supported him, but his chest and limbs were inches deep, motes intermingling. The changes in his body frightened him. The rush of blood in his ears was gone, and so was the thump in his chest. He felt his exertion in his breath. A great volume of air was moving inside him. His lungs had expanded to what had been the borders of his flesh.

When he raised his head, Estra was standing by the bridge, gleaming in the moonlight, looking around, as if there might be others aboard. Above him, wind rusked the billows. On either side, pennants of mist fluttered from the bulwarks.

"I think we're alone," Estra said, turning to face him.

He rose slowly. He could feel the wind on his hip, and as it blew, his legs bowed. The motes shifted, but they didn't drift far; as the wind faded, they returned to their places, and his legs straightened.

"You've changed," she said.

She raised her arms to embrace him, and vapor trailed beneath. The arms lost their lines, became nearly transparent; then they halted and the motes caught up, refilling their hollowed containers. The rounded mount—the ship's bridge—was behind her. Arden could see it through her.

He was speechless, trembling in every part.

Estra's face fell. "Don't panic," she said.

3

Sun flared in Arden's eyes, and when he turned away
from the brightness, a pliant coolness brushed his
ear. His head was resting on a pillow of fog. A quilt
of mist lay over him, its lavender swells sequined with gold.
Estra was seated beside him, watching.

He raised his hand and peered through it.

"Welcome to the intangible." She stood.

He rose slowly, reaching for her. Her hand was feather-soft,
but it helped him steady himself. Gravity—he still felt it. But
standing was more like inflation, being buoyed up.

Mist hid the deck. Scarves and veils were drifting around
them, obscuring the view on all sides. "It will take some getting used to," Estra said.

He didn't answer, and he didn't move.

She lifted her knee. He watched her leg stretch, separate

from the mist and grow a foot at the end. When she set it back down, the foot melted into the mist.

"Try it," she said.

"I feel like I'll fall through."

"You're not as heavy as you think."

He raised his leg and it stretched like hers had. "I'm still human, aren't I?"

"You're a spirit, Arden. You've come home."

He felt very different—sensations were missing. He was high in the sky, so he should have been freezing. He was chilled, a little; but it was like he'd put on a fur coat. Every mote of his body floated in a pocket of air. Gone too were the familiar noises—the twinkle in his ears, the beating of his heart. He was silent now, except for his breath. As the wind entered and left him, it did so with long, low sound.

"The mind can be troubled," Estra said, "and the heart can ache. You can still feel pain. But the physical shackles are much looser."

Arden's motes felt like they were about to uncenter, to cross boundaries they were meant to honor, each floating away on its own.

"You still have a memory of greater weight," she said, "and it's the memory that tells you you're going to fall." She let go of his hand and took a step back. "Come to me."

They were near the port gunnel. Arden looked down, seeing the empty fathoms beneath the ship and a dark ocean far below.

"Come to me," she said again.

Arden lifted his leg from the fog and moved it toward her. He felt himself tipping and his arms shot out, but he didn't fall. He floated. He grabbed Estra's wrist and it compressed to a dowel. As his feet found the deck again, he felt the furred edge of her hip against his. Where was the map for his body? He was no longer sure where he ended and the air began.

The branching frond was visible on Estra's breast, but it looked like white frost now. Their chests were both foggy, and the light passed through. Below his belly was an alarming sight. His organ was gone. Arden touched himself.

"What's happened to me?" He glanced at Estra's groin. The cleft in her mons had vanished.

"Coupling on earth—" Her brows lifted. "It's a clumsy arrangement."

His loss was painless, but the sight stung him. "Will it come back?"

"What if it doesn't?"

"Is this normal up here?"

"In the sky, love is different," she said. "I don't think you'll be disappointed." She looked around her. Then she raised one hand. "We're moving. Can you feel the wind?"

Before Arden answered, she started forward, plowing a path through the mist. Bollards of vapor rose on either side, appearing and disappearing in the boils and glare.

He did his best to follow. His motes hung together, shifting around the axis of his lost spine.

"Fog is sensitive," Estra told him. "Try to calm yourself. Answer its subtlety with all the lightness you know. Glide. Coast. Make your gait fluid, like a bird in flight.

"Everything here is infused with wind. This cloud has a breath, and we breathe along with it. Wind whirls our flesh, inflates our hearts. Wind carries the words from my tongue. Wind rises out of you and rejoins the sky."

Through the mist, Arden saw the side of the rounded mount.

"The Bridge," Estra said.

"Can you steer a cloud?"

"Intention could give us direction," she said, moving past. "But we're going to let the wind carry us. We want to look uninhabited."

A gap appeared in the shifting scarves. Through it, he could see the top of the Bridge: the ship's helm. A new fear rose among the many stirring. If all this was real, was the man in the thunderhead real too?

"Maybe he'll forget," Arden said.

"Ingis won't forget."

He heard the trouble in her voice. Estra had fears of her own.

"The cats are gone," Arden said. "We have a place of our own. And each other." He spoke with all the confidence he could muster.

Estra's eyes fixed on him. He could see gratitude in them, and hope.

As they reached the front of the cloud, the air cleared around them.

"Look at this." She turned and motes sifted loose, swirling like the skirts of a dancer around her waist.

"The Prow," he said. "The other end will be the Stern."

The cloud was floating in a vast expanse, all white and blue, with a golden sun rising before it. Supple bastions, shifting barricades, twisted spires and gaping wells— Every chink let a morning beam through, and beyond the glittering maze lay an amorphous blanket, level and fleecy, waiting to be shaped.

"It's enough just to breathe, isn't it?" Estra spread her arms, as if contentment was a miraculous thing. "Do you feel free now?"

Her voice, so soft and uncertain— Her beautiful face, framed by the shifting clouds. There was frailty here, unlike anything he'd known on earth.

"I do," Arden said. The sky seemed infinite. There was nothing to bound it.

"Our cloud is like the *Mariod*," she offered.

"It is," he nodded.

"You're not hungry?"

"No."

The ship's stem hit a swell, and the icy spray traveled through him. He turned away from the Prow, seeing the sun and the breeze had stripped the cloud's veils away. The gunnels curved back to the Stern. Above, sheets of fog hung from the masts, luffing and swelling.

"Let's explore," Estra said.

She stepped over the quilted surface and crossed in front of the Bridge, headed to starboard. Arden followed. The vapor parted to admit them, leaving smooth-sided banks that compressed and whorled, resealing as they passed.

"You've been on a cloud like this?"

"They're all a bit different," she said. "And they're always changing."

The way sloped down. As they descended, the mist settled.

"Look. It's glittering," Estra said.

The surface was level before them, reflecting the sun like a noonday beach.

"It's flat as a deck," he observed.

Estra turned. "The Glitter Deck," they said together.

She started across it, and when she reached the gunnels, Arden coasted beside her. Over the curled edge, he could see a vastness of sky, and waters below.

"Smell." She drew a gust in, and he did the same.

A tang of salt hung in the air.

"He must have been crazy," Arden said, "to drive you away."

Estra bowed her head.

"I know how lucky I am to be with you," he said.

The morning glow lit the motes of her face. "Two days ago," she said, "my life was hopeless. I keep thinking, 'I fell into his arms. He was waiting to catch me.'"

He touched her middle, and his finger slid into it.

"Look there." Estra pointed aft.

Swells of haze mounted to dunes, and the dunes ascended

to motionless hills. Here was a softness and airiness no ship ever had.

"They'll be our Lofts." Estra smiled.

She crossed the Glitter Deck and hurried through the dunes, leaving a sinuous trail, like a finger passing through loose sugar. "You'll like this place," she said with delight in her voice.

The Lofts were plush and soft as oakum. The fog around them was thicker here, and the sun was higher. As weightless as Arden felt, he seemed to be growing lighter.

"There's nothing on earth like this," she said.

Motes lifted from Estra's face. Motes in layers—masks of care, each a bit different, each drifting away. Arden was sloughing atoms from his head and chest, like a fungus sheds spores.

"Every fair-weather cloud has a calm spot," she said.

"Estra—"

"I'm remembering," she said, "my fair-weather faith."

"Faith?" The sun's heat was leavening what remained of him, warming his motes, pulling them apart. He was losing definition, growing more translucent.

"There was something before us," she said. "The first breath of the cosmos, the warmth that first blessed us, the breast that first fed us the wondrous fog."

"People don't speak this way to each other."

"They don't," she agreed. "But we're no longer people."

"I'm too light—"

Estra drew closer. Their borders overlapped. "What is freedom?" she said. "Who are we really, when we're free?"

57

"I'm sorry—"

"What's the matter?"

"I feel like I'm losing myself."

"That's part of the sky's magic." Her eyes darted, searching. "It's what the soul wants. And it's practice for love. Giving yourself to another. Remember Mariod—her care, her devotion— The love she poured into you, like cream down the throat of a white orchid."

"She's gone," he said. "She's been gone a long time."

"The child is still there, smiling and crying inside you."

"I'm not ready for this." Arden scanned the Lofts, shuddered and turned his back on them, shifting his legs slowly. Estra moved beside him.

"We have time," she said. "I'm sorry. I don't mean to—"

"I've been a toiler all my life," he said. "Wanting. Not having."

"I know."

"The one person I loved— I cried when she kissed me goodbye. I screamed when I saw what was left. Every night, I prayed she'd come back."

"You don't believe life can be kind," Estra said.

"I want to be here. I want to be with you. I want to be free."

"It's a matter of trust," she said, "isn't it. When things are uncertain, you fear the worst. I understand. I have fears too. I smother them. I bury them deep inside me. And then, when I'm not expecting, they rise up and pierce my heart."

"As long as I worked on my boat," he said, "I dreamt of

failure. In my dreams, they found me out—in the forest, hauling the *Mariod* down to the bay, on the shore as I was about to launch her. They carried me back. I was soaked and tortured. My nights were filled with punishments. Will the nights here be any different?"

He took a breath. They were out of the Lofts. He was denser and more opaque. "It's always with me: the curse of being powerless."

"Everyone has failures, Arden."

"You're talking about Ingis."

She turned her head. "I was happy here once."

"I can see that."

"My heart and mind—" She swallowed her words.

"You said you were never in love with him. That's not true, is it."

She sighed and shook her head. "We had something, but he destroyed it."

Arden looked into her eyes. "I don't know what's going on in your head."

"You could ask me."

"Are you thinking about him?"

"No."

"You're saying that to spare my feelings."

"I don't care about Ingis," she insisted, scanning the sky, as if trying to see a way out of their plight. "I came here with such high hopes, and this beautiful world ended up being a torment to me."

A tear appeared on Estra's cheek. It vanished as he watched, like a raindrop in the sea. "Forgive me," he said. "I wish I was stronger, nobler—"

"You're right. It's true. I've been thinking of him. I've been fearful too, and angry the memories won't leave me.

"Your thirst for freedom— When you spoke of it on earth, my spirit soared. And now—we're here. But freedom frightens me too. The mind can justify anything." Her eyes searched his. "Where will freedom lead you? To inspiration? To hope and love? Other desires are lurking inside us. You can cut your moorings, free yourself from an imprisoning world. But your desires go with you."

"I want to be loved," he said, "by someone like you."

"Someone." Her voice sank. "I'm poisoned, Arden. Poisoned with anger and all the abuse I endured. When his thoughts are labored, I am the midwife. When they're weighted with guilt, I ease his load. When rage shorts his circuits, I take the blame. I'm his better, his confessor. His concubine, his whore. I'm food when there is nothing to eat." Estra shook her head. "We need a vat."

"A vat?"

"To flush the misery of bondage out of your system," she said. "And to wash away my anger at Ingis. We can't make this ship our home until we've done that."

A pole of fog turned in the wind, rising from behind the Bridge like a mainmast. Estra and Arden stood by the pole's collar, gazing up. She put her arms to her sides, flexed her legs and pushed off.

Estra rose into the air, spreading her arms, toes pointed down, turning a slow spiral around the mast. As she reached its top, she sculled, slowing and circling, scouting the cloud fore and aft. Then she tucked and rolled, diving back down.

"We have one," she said when she was back beside him. She gasped with relief. "And there are Spindles nearby."

The Vat was at the top of a swell. The cloud had cracked around it, and the perimeter was littered with puffs. Estra halted before it.

"Careful," she said. "Have a look, but keep your balance."

Arden approached the rim. The Vat was twenty feet across and full of fog. The surface was whirling, furrowed and spiral-striped, gray and black, with an ebony pock at its center.

"We're going in?"

"For a few seconds," she said, "and not together. You'll go first. I'll pull you out."

"What does it do?"

"It will wash away memories. One of the sky's sorceries." She regarded the Vat with respect. "There's some guesswork. Memories are tricky things."

She edged against him, putting her hand on his loin. "Those at the front of your mind go first. Focus on the things you want to forget. Think about the sorrows of being a toiler. Fill your mind with the memories that harry you. Don't let your mind wander."

Arden eyed the dark whorls. They were corded and foaming, and the center sucked with intent.

"Concentrate," Estra said. "Your mind is full of memories you don't want to lose. Rest your middle on the rim and ease yourself in. The solvent weights you, so levitation's impossible. Keep one hand above the surface. I'll count to four, then I'll pull you out."

Arden faced her, seeing a blink of fear.

"The length of time matters," she said. "It starts here," she touched her hairline, "and works its way down. The longer you're in, the deeper the wash."

He remembered the night he and Mariod were led to Apex.

Estra's brow creased. "Let's make it three. I'll count to three."

He nodded.

"One, two, three," she prepped him. "Keep your hand up. You'll feel me grab it. We don't want to erase too much."

"One, two, three," he murmured.

She moved to one side.

Arden squared himself and faced the gyre. He could hear Estra's breath in his ear. He put his hands on the rim, composed himself and curled his trunk over it. Then he dipped his head down, loosened his grip and plunged in.

His mind blanked as the cold took hold. He forced his attention back—blood, wounds, the sting of humiliation— The thoughts were like slippery fish. He was moving, face down. The spiraling surface admitted some light, enough that he could see into the Vat. It was smooth-sided and funnel-shaped. He raised his right arm.

"One," Estra counted.

As the whorls swept through his mind, he saw, he remembered, reliving the pain. Priests in their robes; the one he loved best, her face blackened and smoking. Hunted by hounds, beaten, shivering in Soak.

"Two."

Desperate wishes, hopeless hopes. Aching, heartsick and shaking; the city on a hill, and in every window, the staring souls.

"Three."

His mind clouded, his vision gave out. In the darkness, curls glowed, curls and circles, circles and spirals where the evils had nested.

"I'm here," Estra said.

The curls and circles began to slow. They broke into hooks and crescents that dimmed and shrank. He opened his eyes, seeing Estra's face with the sun behind her.

"Who am I?" she said.

"My salvation."

Estra laughed.

He raised himself slowly. He was lying amid the puffs beside the Vat. Over Estra's shoulder, the mizzenmast rose, sheets of fog hanging from its spars. A raft of mist floated beyond the port gunnels. He could measure their progress against it. The cloud had a razor clarity. And his servitude— The memories were dim now, and the pain was gone. It had been a long dream, a bad one, and he had finally awoken.

"What was it like, back on earth?"

"I'm not thinking about that," he said, touching her cheek.

"One," Arden counted, his eyes fixed on Estra. She was bobbing on the Vat's furrowed surface, circling on her side like a flitch of half-rendered fat. "Two. Three."

He hooked his arms beneath her shoulders and pulled. Her neck compressed and her torso stretched.

Estra's chest emerged, then her waist. Her knee caught on the rim, and his left arm came loose. Arden yelled, caught her and hauled her over the rim.

She was cold and her eyes were closed, but he saw breath in her nostrils. A shadowy tide waxed through her translucent chest. He lay her down and stretched beside her, pressing her close.

She grew warmer. Her breath deepened, and her motes seemed to pack together. Finally, her lids parted.

Her eyes had a wondering look.

"We're on our cloud," he said.

She fixed on him, frowning. She raised her shoulder, eyeing her body, as if it was strange to her.

"You were in the Vat."

She squinted. "Arden."

He nodded.

She looked around her, and the breeze blew off her frown. It hovered like a mask in the air between them, and then the motes of her face were reshaping.

"I'm better," she said. "Much better. Will you help me up?"

He rose with her.

"You've been in?" she said.

"Yes. I'm better too."

"I'm so glad." She opened her arms, and he did the same, and their bodies lapped over each other, motes intermingling. Arden heard her tears. Tears of relief, grateful tears. Her brow met his, and they shared them.

The Vat had purged their demons, he thought.

"The past isn't love," Estra said. "Love is the future."

They stood there, holding each other. Then Estra led him to the Spindles, where—she said—those who live in the clouds sometimes go, after a rinse in the Vat.

Through veils of mist, cones appeared in a murky hollow—cones of vapor, turning slowly, each at a different speed. Estra led Arden among them. They were twisted and spiraled, and they gave off puffs of vapor as they turned. The tallest were at the hollow's center. What was their purpose? How long had the cones been turning?

"A mournful place," he said.

"Here, wishes can't hide. You can see them."

Estra halted before a cone twice her height and turned to face him. "You're not afraid," she said. "You want to know." She was asking for his assent.

"I trust you," he said.

She kissed him. Then she raised her hand and brushed his chest. As he watched, she pushed her fingers into it.

"Above your heart," she said. "An odd little thing, like a piece of lint." Her brow furrowed. "I've got it."

Arden felt a tugging.

"Here it comes." Estra's fingers emerged with a cord of fog, twisted and raveling. It twitched in the air before him, like a seeking sprout.

She continued to pull, drawing it through the motes of his sternum.

"Ready?" she said.

She touched the cord's end to the turning spindle, and the spindle caught hold of it. As the spindle turned, the cord wound around.

Now Estra reached inside her own chest, facing the cone beside his. She pulled out a frayed leader and attached it.

"The Spindles are wish collectors," she said, watching hers turn.

"They make wishes come true?"

"No," she said. "They can only reveal them."

Arden felt it moving inside him, like a rill of ice water. Before him, dew dripped from the taut cord. As the cone spooled it up, the cord ticked like a clock. His heart throbbed, racing, unruly—resisting. Where the cord spooled round the cone, a mist was rising, greenish and glittering, filling the air with the wish hidden inside him. He could see it now; he could feel its need and sense its meaning. Why was his heart so unwilling?

Estra began to whimper, softly, to herself. She was peering at her own green cloud, with longing, with sorrow and hope.

"What does the spindle tell you?" she asked.

His continued to drag out the cord, but he knew the answer.

"I wish for courage in love," he said. "To be brave enough to receive it."

The hollow resounded with his declaration.

"I wish for modesty in love," Estra said. "Purity and contentment."

The spindles let go of the wishing lines, and their hearts snatched them back. The loose end of Arden's line whipped and vanished into his chest.

He turned, regarding her through the green glitter.

"Simple wishes," he said.

"I see now the reason for our attraction." Estra moved closer, searching his face. "You imagined I could grant your wish. And I imagined you could grant mine. Life went wrong for us, but things have changed."

She cocked her head, hesitant, as if she had something to hide.

"I got a glimpse of the future," she said, "at the top of the mast. Our future together, here on this cloud."

"What do you mean?"

"We have a lake," she said. "A small one."

Arden waited. Estra's manner had changed. She seemed resolute, determined.

"You were born with a gift," she said.

Arden shook his head, unable to guess her meaning.

"Candor," she said. "Truth. Deep feelings—the deepest."

"I don't understand."

"You're going to declare them," she said, "and I'm going to help."

"Declare them?"

"With words," she said, "like those you wrote on the back of Mariod's portrait."

"I have no skill—"

Estra motioned. "Follow me."

The little lake was midway between bow and stern, near the starboard bulwarks.

"The Pond," Arden said when it came into view.

It was gleaming and kidney-shaped, at the bottom of a foggy incline. They descended side by side. The cloud was running downwind now, pennants flying from mast and rail.

"I've never written anything for anyone else."

"It will all be private, just for you and me."

"What will I say?"

"We'll find out."

68

White tufts idled around the Pond's rim. As they approached, the pearling surface grew rings and eyes.

Estra surveyed the shore by the water's edge. "Why don't you sit here."

Arden lowered himself onto a pallet of fog. She sat beside him.

The Pond was an uneven mirror. He could see the warped reflection of a school of scuds drifting by. Estra reached with her arm, gathering mist from the margin and sweeping it toward them, spreading it evenly over the surface.

She glanced at him. "There's our paper."

Arden laughed. He pointed his forefinger, set it down on the "paper" and scribed the letter *E*. The skim of mist took the impression.

"Wonderful," she said, edging closer.

"I'm going to need your help."

"I'll whisper encouragements in your ear."

"I'll need more help than that," he said.

"We'll work on the ideas together. I'll stir your emotions. I'm good at that. I loved what you wrote about Mariod," she said. "Let's start with something romantic."

"Something short," he said.

"We have plenty of time."

Arden looked up. The sun was directly above them. Below it, cirrus hoods—windblown cowls—were dragging across the sky.

"'The Night We Met,'" he said.

"Perfect."

He hunched over the misty page, casting for an entry. Estra watched.

She was wet, he wrote, *shivering.* He stared at the silver-gray sheet. *I could barely hear her over the rain.*

He looked up. "I thought you were going to help me."

"You were bold," she said. "You picked me up and carried me into your shelter."

"I don't think this will work."

"What's wrong?"

"It doesn't feel natural to me," he said gently.

"Be patient," she said. "Please."

I picked her up, he wrote, *and carried her into my shelter.*

He paused.

I felt bolb— Arden winced. He used the heel of his hand to erase the mistake, but the movement blurred all the words on the page.

"I'm sorry." He knew he was disappointing her.

"Don't be." She kissed his shoulder.

"I'm not a poet. I dig culverts. I repair sluices. It took me years to make my boat."

"I just know," Estra said. "Our wishes will find their fulfillment here."

"If I had learned—"

"I want you to bare your soul to me, Arden. And I'm going to bare mine to you. Here. We'll talk about love, and we'll find your courage. I know it's there. And— I'll tell you about my struggle for peace. For contentment. With you, I'm going to find it." Her smile was tentative. "Is that too soppy?"

Arden shook his head.

"I can start things," she offered. "I'm not a poet either. But let's see how I do."

She rested her chin on his shoulder and put her lips to his ear.

"*I was desperate that night,*" she said. "*Frightened and alone.* Go on. Don't worry about legibility.

"*How could it be? The love I'd dreamt of and longed for—Eager and close, holding me? Ready to blind himself to everything else and sail away.* You'll need to write faster if you're going to keep up. Don't think about the words. Just let them flow through your finger. Here. This will help."

She leaned her head against his, and their atomized brows overlapped. When she resumed speaking, her voice seemed like his own.

Estra's words were naked, rich with emotion. A breeze shunted the page as Arden wrote. Her voice slowed and then raced, was gentle then forced, grave and lighthearted. His confidence mounted. She paused, reaching for a thought but not finding, and he jumped in. Words poured from his lips—or were they hers again?

"*That unforgettable night. A night of ardor. A night of questions. To find our freedom and live for love, only for love—what would that mean? We would be creators. Love would be a new kind of expression. We would devote ourselves, spend ourselves, lose ourselves in our creation.*"

"A new kind of expression," Arden repeated.

He raised his finger from the Pond.

71

"It's done," Estra said.

Using her fingers, she peeled the sheet off, and as Arden watched, the feathered edges curled and turned into wings. A large crane, silver-gray, lifted from the surface, neck reaching, legs trailing back. The words were visible on its wings, each line on a pinion. The crane rose with a stuttering cry, its long beak aimed, climbing quickly.

Arden was amazed. "You knew—"

"Let's just say I expected." Estra leaned back.

Together they followed the bird as it circled over them.

"Only love can do that," she said. "Shall we go again?"

"What's next?"

"How we left the earth. What we found on our cloud."

The hours flew by. To Arden's surprise, Estra's energy didn't flag. And his focus didn't waver. When a page was complete, she stripped it from the Pond and released it into the sky. Then she curried a fresh layer of mist over the mirror and they started on another.

They created cranes to honor their tie, then they took up more arcane and fanciful things. Secrets—buried, never before shared. Somnolent thoughts, dreamy, narcotic. A mad impulse, an unaccountable dream, an obsession with name. His finger raced, her lips moved like mumbling in sleep.

My deliverance, my soul, the sacred five letters. At dawn, I'll see them climbing above the horizon. At twilight, I'll paint them across the sky. At midnight, I will write them with the tip of my tongue on your thigh.

Arden, the name—its tuck and glide—wrings dew from my heart and pearls from my eyes.

By sundown, a small flock of cranes circled the ship.

Arden's eyes burned. Estra's breath was steaming.

She rose, watching the birds, listening to their stuttering cries. "Not a word we've written is false," she said.

He raised himself, admiring the cranes in flight. He would never have imagined their efforts at the Pond would turn out so well.

"We're different now," he said. And when she met his gaze, he could tell: she knew what he meant. Where their heads had mingled, a new mind had been born.

They stood side by side, regarding their reflection in the watery mirror.

"Your words fill the air," he said. "But I see them here too." He touched his chest. "You have written on me."

"And you see," Estra put her hand on her breast, "what being your muse has done. This lonely soul finally has a mate."

They studied their reflection in silence, then they turned and started up the slope.

"Will there ever be a day like this again?" Arden said.

"They will all be like this," Estra replied.

When they reached the Spindles, it was dusk and the hollow was dim. Estra found a trundle of fog and was patting it down. "We can sleep here tonight."

"What is that?" Arden said.

On the rim of the hollow was an unexpected sight. A large curl had risen and was frozen there, like the back of a band shell, stained coral by the raking light.

Estra gave him a mystified look.

"It wasn't there this morning," he said.

They wound their way through the rotating cones, and when they reached the Band Shell, they circled it. A rippling terrace appeared, and there were puffs like bolstered divans on either side. Beneath the front of the Band Shell, a mesh of mist was suspended: a hammock strung amid colored smokes.

They crossed the terrace to a pair of misty veils hanging like drapery. Estra parted them. They were standing by the port bulwarks, staring into space.

Arden leaned over the gunnel and looked down. There was land far below, dun-colored plateaus with eroded slopes. The cloud was gliding effortlessly. Its hull was sleek, without joints or planking.

She turned away from the view. "A bower," she said, scanning the space. "Made for us."

They approached the hammock together.

Estra steadied the mesh and eased herself down. Beneath the Band Shell, the shadows were thick. "Perfect," she sighed, and a small plume of steam emerged from her lips.

Arden lay on his back beside her, the mesh stretching beneath him.

At the Pond, all had seemed stable; but here, things were shifting. The Band Shell trembled. A wave crossed the terrace. The misty drapes opened and closed on their own.

A breeze passed, and the hammock began to sway.

He rolled onto his hip, facing Estra. The ship would drift while they were asleep, at the mercy of winds, however they blew. The thought was unsettling.

As if to comfort him, she put her lips to his. He felt a sting of frost in the kiss, and as they nestled together, the fog thickened. The divans blurred, and so did the terrace. The ship was breathing, and the Bower along with it, every surface stirred by the wind's infusions.

"We'll spend our lives here," Estra said.

"How long do we have?"

"As long as we would on earth. If no misfortune intervenes."

"There's a natural end?"

She nodded. "Your motes won't change, but your will weakens until it's unable to hold them together." She raised her hand, covering her yawn with her fingers. Then she edged against him.

Her cheek softened, her shoulder, her hip— She was joining the mist, and so was he. His limbs evanesced, then his waist and his chest.

"A solitary dream is an illusion," she said. "But a dream that two share is real."

Then their heads met, as they had at the Pond, and the voice seemed his own. The voice and the thought.

The ship cruised into the darkness, losing its borders. The stars winked and disappeared.

4

They stood at the Prow as the sun rose, watching puffs of down float by.

"I'm glad to be alive," Arden rasped. His throat was raw from all the fog he'd inhaled the previous night.

Estra's eyes were slitted, blissful.

He turned his face up. "How high the sky is," he swung toward the stern, "and how clear in all directions." He could see the swollen sheets of the Mainmast, and amidship, the vacant Bridge. "Any idea where we're headed?"

"Ask the wind," Estra said.

He looked down. They were over water again—a sea dotted with islands. And there was a coast in the distance. Peaks with sharp edges. "Shouldn't we know?"

"You've been thinking about that?"

"Not really. But—"

"But what?"

"Don't we care? Doesn't the ship need a pilot?"

"No. It doesn't."

Her voice was brittle.

"Just be happy we're drifting," Estra said. "There's a danger in plotting a course."

"Because of Ingis."

She nodded. "And because of us."

"What are you afraid of?"

She gazed at the Bridge. "Maybe we'll wake up one morning, and the helm will be gone." Her eyes were dark. "You don't understand these things."

"You're upset with me."

"I'm not," she shook her head. "You never know where being purposeful will lead, Arden. You're thinking of the goal, you're convinced you're on course. And then you realize: by forgetting 'right here' and 'right now,' you've lost everything. You and I— We've chanced on something precious. Let's keep our attention on *that*. The goal isn't out there. It's in here." She touched the frond-shaped scar over her heart.

He felt her sincerity and the truth in her words. "I'm with you," he said.

Arden turned, gazing in the direction of the Pond. "We spoke with one voice yesterday. Will we find that harmony again?"

She smiled. "Let's try."

Beneath a vault of blue sky, with the sun perfectly round overhead, the gunnels glitter and the jacklines flash; our deck gleams and there's a winking star on our Prow. The ship is fit, ready for whatever lies ahead.

What more can we ask for?

Without a home port, without charts or compass, and with no way to signal any other craft on the sea— No anchorage in creation will ever cheer our arrival.

With no flanking clouds to measure our progress, we might be motionless. Are we caught on a reef? Grounded in a shallow? Or foundering and sinking into the deep? Perhaps we have no destination. Our sails are full and our nose cuts the waves, but we are making no headway at all.

You laugh and I kiss you. We both know better.

On this ship of ours, we are traveling into each other. My hand is on the wheel, and there's a beacon in your eyes. Night and day, we gain the distance together, feeling our way toward the far harbor of the soul.

Estra slid her fingers beneath the skin of mist and lifted, and the wings of a silver crane curled up, batting fiercely, rising into the air.

She sighed and reseated herself. "'The True Destination.'"

"It turned out well," Arden said.

On arriving at the Pond an hour before, he had searched the sky.

"Our cranes are gone," he had said.

"They're right in front of you." Estra directed his gaze.

The cranes were standing in the water with their wings scrolled around them. Their thin legs rose from rippling targets. They had spent the night there.

"Keep your voice low," she said, "and try not to stare."

Her words surprised him. He approached the verge slowly, leading the way. The cranes muttered to each other, following his movements closely, as if they mistrusted him. Did they not understand? They were his own thoughts and feelings.

"It's alright," Estra said. "They know who you are."

The cranes seemed on edge, but they didn't scatter.

He and Estra seated themselves. The birds continued to watch them, conferring in an alien tongue.

"They have lives of their own now," Estra whispered.

"You know a lot about them."

She looked aside. "You're forgetting how long I've lived in the sky."

The hours passed quickly. The cranes circled above or stood watching nearby. By the end of the day, Arden knew what to expect. Despite their detachment, he felt a kinship with them. They brought poise and dignity to the Pond, and as the page count mounted, their nature seeped into the lines he and Estra were writing.

"They understand the flight of the spirit that you and I are taking."

She nodded. "And they share our desire for a private life."

When he and Estra rose to depart, the roosting cranes lifted as one, filling the air with stuttering cries. He glanced at Estra, but she was gazing past them, scanning the sky, checking in every direction. She saw he was watching her, and she smiled, acting carefree. "Look where we are," she said, as if she'd been marveling at their good fortune.

As they approached the Band Shell, the sun was sinking. The west-facing bulwarks sparkled, and rivulets trenched down from the Lofts, flowing over the stern, leaving a wake that hissed and coiled.

On the terrace Arden faced her. "Can we make love tonight?"

She smiled and seated herself on the hammock. "Of course."

He lowered himself beside her. "How is it done?"

"It's easy. Effortless." She stretched out. "Lie down."

Arden lay on his side, circled her with his arm and peered into her sage eyes.

The sun was compressing on the horizon, like a ball of peach-colored sap.

"It's like what we do at the Pond," she explained. "You lean together, but farther. Until there's only one of us."

Arden digested her words. Then he took a breath and moved closer.

He felt their chests touch and mingle, then the keels of their hips, and the tops of their thighs. The lapped surfaces tingled—a pleasurable sensation he was accustomed to now.

"Closer," she whispered. Her cheek touched his.

"Will it be like—"

"You'll see."

The motes of their legs shared the same space now. Their chests were half-overlapped.

"Closer," she whispered.

Their groins merged—not grossly as they might have on earth, but particle by particle, with the fineness and equality of mist. The amplitude of the tingling mounted, ringing through Arden's core. He could feel the motes of his innards now, joining hers. His breath was his own; and then, all at once, it was shared. Their chests were inflating together, and their gasps were united.

He felt lighter. Had a sudden wind filled the ghost ship's sails? He and Estra were rising together—two spirits. Or one.

"Our heads now," she whispered.

Estra's cheek felt muzzy. Her chin ebbed. As he pressed his temple to hers, Estra's brow floated over her eye. "Closer," she whispered, "closer—"

Her voice spoke from outside him; and then it was enormous, inside his ear, stark and immediate.

You are what I want from life, he thought. *All I have ever wanted.*

Estra could hear.

A sudden cloudburst shook them, blessing their union with rain. And then a great midnight husk opened above them, and stars fell in thick clouds. Twinkling stars, cosmic beads, lustering motes and atomic tears— As the thick brew churned and drowned them, Arden felt his last refuge eroding, the final asylum, the last lonely cell of a forlorn soul— Fearing the void, he sobbed and recanted. His heart shrank and withdrew.

And then—

All their motes merged, condensing in a silver fluid, teeming with words.

I'm yours, I'm yours, I'm completely yours—

Without voice or pen-finger, without ears or throat, the purest elixir of love flowed out: a crystal water that painted the night with great loops and flourishes, wild jots and curls— beautiful, devastating, heart-stopping words.

In the days that followed, they threw themselves at the Pond and each other. They merged their motes when the impulse struck them, not just in the hammock or at the close of day. At the Prow, by the Mainmast, in the Lofts or the stern— Birthing cranes, too, kept no schedule. Before sunrise, in the late hours, whenever an idea seized them, they hurried to the Pond and raised a new bird from a heartfelt page.

They shared every thought, every feeling, it seemed. Had their minds become one? There were no unlit corners, he thought. No silent pockets, nothing out of reach or hidden from view. Estra's voice softened with each passing day, and Arden embraced the hush, as if their new life was a secret that mustn't get out. The ship became a place of silence and whispers.

They levitated often. One bright morning, they circled

over the bows, and then floated alongside the starboard gunnels, singing Mariod's song and rolling over and over, while a barren land passed beneath them. Arden noticed a spot that was hived and sectored. When he asked, Estra was reluctant to answer and looked away. But when he pressed her, she named the dead metropolis and pointed out two large craters where bombs had dropped.

The cranes numbered in the scores now. They were increasingly independent, and Arden accepted that. When it came to being observed, the cranes were insistent. If either were watching, the birds would take flight. Estra no longer had to peel them from the Pond. A new crane would raise itself with a *cuck* of triumph, once it felt complete. And the birds had opinions about how they'd been fashioned. The reckless style displeased them. They objected to frenzied proclamations, and they would settle on the shore and preen them away. They preferred weighty words, solemn and reverent, with a deliberate rhythm.

The cranes caballed with each other, circling over them while they worked, roosting while they slept. Awkward as they were, stilted in the water, they were miracles of grace in the air. A frictionless wheel, a gliding snake, a dipping bough with silver blades—

What a shock it was when they disappeared.

Arden and Estra were at the Pond. It was midafternoon, and there was nothing between them and the sun. To reduce the glare, Estra shifted beside him, keeping her shadow over the page. Arden listened and wrote.

Dew stipples our decks. A needle of sun pierces the quilting. The wind huffs, the masts groan. The sheets stretch as the wind drives into them, and their collars rumple as the wind draws out. A sugary arch appears over our bows, doughy, twisting. We torpedo through it, skeins clinging, trailing from our gunnels like tangled silks.

There's force in the wind, fury in the tumbling combers. Force and fury, and clashing motes, whirling pearls, shattered diamonds— From the cruel churning, its icy heart, from the merciless roils rise fever jags, twitching twigs, glittering thistles.

Arden lifted his finger. "You're so well-spoken."

Estra seemed not to hear. She was eyeing the words on the skim of mist, looking troubled, frightened.

The pinions shifted. The crane's wings rose and flexed, about to lift off. Then bursts of fire sprang from the lines. Hissing wires, flashing thorns— Some of the words were glowing, smoking.

Estra's eyes were wide.

As Arden watched, the fiery words burnt holes in the crane's wings, and the batting ceased. The bird was nothing more than a burnt page now, falling to pieces, its ashes dissolving back into the mist of the Pond.

Arden gazed at Estra, trying to understand what had happened.

"My mind was wandering," she said numbly.

The cranes were rigid, standing on the shore, staring at her with alarm. She whimpered and raised her hand, as if to hide herself from them. One squawked and raised its wings, and then the others joined in, railing at her and jabbering to each other.

Arden stood, reaching for Estra. "Leave her alone," he yelled at the birds.

The cranes froze. They turned their united stare on him, mute and severe, silver fetishes inlaid with mother-of-pearl. Then their beaks opened, and the air was full of stuttering cries. Wings spread and the cranes lifted into the air, rising over the Pond, banking together.

Estra watched, looking resigned.

A pair of birds flew past, wings beating as one. Arden felt the downdraft and heard their whispering primaries. The flock rose in formation, sideslipped to port and cleared the gunnels, an S at first, straightening to an I.

"Where are they going?" he wondered.

The cranes were sculling deeply, long necks aimed. They arrowed between two cumulus turrets and trailed into a stratus banded peach and teal, sharing their ideas about the route and the sky.

"Our words," he said weakly, watching the birds disappear.

Estra didn't reply.

His ear clung to the stutter. Slowly it faded.

The cranes had been wary of them, but Arden had thought they were bound to the ship. What had caused the page to catch fire? What was it about the burning crane that had so alarmed the others? Had Arden's outburst frightened them off? When he turned to Estra, she looked away. Troubled. Pained, perhaps. Alone with herself.

"What happened?" he said, regarding the Pond. "Where are they going, with our words on their wings?"

Estra gazed at him. "They may come back."

She sounded as if their return might be something to dread.

The next day, the ship was becalmed, swamped by fog. The winds died, and the sun was blotted. The two of them walked the decks. Estra was still in eclipse. Their perceptions, Arden thought. Their labor together— There was nothing to show for it. The cloud seemed deserted. They stopped at the Pond, eyeing the shore where the cranes had roosted. Then, without uttering a word, they returned to the Bower.

As they stepped onto the terrace, he faced her. "What does it matter. We have the life we wished for." He touched his chest. "The spirit that moves inside us—that's what counts."

Estra smiled. He put his arms around her. Since they'd been on the ghost ship, so many thoughts and feelings—worthy, earnest—had passed between them.

"We should be content," he said.

"Yes, we should."

"Our last crane," he said. "That upset you, didn't it."

Estra was silent.

"Its electricity frightened you."

"No." She shook her head.

"Can I ask you something?"

Estra regarded him.

"At the Spindles—" He paused. "I'm still puzzled."

"About what?"

"Why modesty would be so important to you."

She bowed her head. "Freedom in the sky— All the things we want— I worry that it's . . . too much. More isn't always better. My wish was to be happy with less."

"Look," he pointed.

Wands of dawn pierced the mist, spotting the terrace.

"For you," he said, pulling her into the light. "To put the glow back in your eyes."

Estra laughed.

Over the Lofts, the sun appeared, bobbing in a sea of fog.

"Today," Arden said, "will be a modest day. No wild feelings, no feverish expression." He nodded at the hammock and led her toward it. "We'll be idle. We'll take slow breaths and think long thoughts."

There was thanks in her eyes. "We won't tempt desire," she said.

"It will have to find its way to us."

As they lay down in the hammock, the sun sprang from the froth. The Band Shell, the terrace—everything was dazzling, painfully bright.

Arden kissed her ear. "The Modest Day has begun."

She reached her hand out and wiggled her fingers. "I can feel its warmth."

"Gently," he warned her. "Give it time to accept us."

Silence. Measured breaths.

"Now," Arden said. "The Day is ready."

Estra nestled against him. "It's like sinking into a summer pool."

Once the Modest Day was around them, they could see the sky as the Day did. Through narrowed lids, it was swimmy and tilted. A field of white puffs—hundreds of them—tumbled in slow-motion down a gentle slope. An illusion perhaps. Perhaps the white puffs were idling in place, while the Modest Day—with both of them in it—slid past.

Did it matter? Not to the Day. It was content to call everything a trifle, even its own splendor.

At noon, the sun slid behind a mist, and the muffled light tinted the sky. Long pink clouds lay side by side like fish steaks on a blue platter. Then slowly, ever so slowly, the sun declined. As it approached the horizon, it settled behind a bank of fog.

"Naked, the sun is blinding," Arden said. "Through the fog we see it clearly. It's the same with love. In the calm we know another's soul."

A modest smile rose to Estra's lips, and sank back into her. "If I were dead," she said, "if you could only love me as a ghost, a woman living an afterlife— Would you still want me?"

Just then, the wind picked up, and the air turned cold. The sky darkened abruptly and rain began to fall. Arden saw the germ of fear in Estra's eyes.

Something drubbed the bows. A stiff wind shook the Band Shell, and the hammock lurched.

Estra stood, turning her head, face twitching.

"What's wrong?" Arden rose.

"Thunder."

A faint rumbling sounded in the distance.

Estra hurried across the terrace. He followed. She parted the gauzy drapes, and together they scanned the leagues of air.

"It's him," Estra said.

"Are you sure?"

A storm cloud was visible, ten degrees off their Prow. It rose on a narrow neck, its black head high in the sky, with an anvil-shaped crown, blown back by the wind.

"That's Ingis," she said.

Arden felt the claws of fear digging in, dragging him back. He was a child again, watching the rain god destroyer advance. A thunderhead, like a nuclear blast. "Are you sure?"

The storm was a long way off, and an inland waterway lay between them. Its billows were lit by interior flashes.

"Every time he strikes," Estra said, "I think, 'A soul's been consumed.'"

Her dread sharpened his own. White wires emerged from the black boils, reaching through space, feeling forward.

"We're headed straight toward him," she said.

She hurried from the Bower, and Arden followed. As she approached the lower story of the Bridge, she slowed.

"What are we doing?" he asked.

She gazed up at the mount. "I'm not sure." Estra closed her eyes and took a breath. Then she shook her head, put her arms to her sides and kicked off, levitating up.

Arden did the same, and they arrived on the mount together.

The Bridge was a cockpit of sorts—a foggy enclosure open to the sky. Its curbs were swirling, white and icy, and a wavering beam on the forward side looked like a rail carved from bone.

"It's never been used," Estra muttered. She stepped forward and put her hands on the rail, raising her chin. "I was a fool." Her face tensed, and the motes of her brow and temples began to squirm.

Arden could feel the ship turning.

"What are you doing?"

Estra didn't reply.

"Talk to me," Arden said.

"I'm sorry. I really am." Estra glanced to port. "The wind's carrying us toward him. We don't have any choice."

Ingis was ninety degrees off the starboard gunnels now, and the ship was still turning. "You make it look easy."

"Fair-weather clouds are meek," Estra said. "They have winds inside them, and the winds serve whoever is at the helm." She spoke the words grimly.

The ship completed its turn, showing the storm cloud its stern.

"Has he spotted us?" Arden wondered.

"You can help. Put your hands on the rail. That thatch of cirrus, glowing like brass? I'm fixing on that."

Arden grasped the rail.

"Concentrate," Estra said. "Send your thoughts forward."

He could feel the Prow's keenness, and Estra's seeking— her focused intention.

"Don't think about me," she said, "and don't think about now. The ship will slow, and we'll be drifting again. Keep your eye on that glow. Keep your mind on the goal."

A flicker and a flash behind them. The rumble echoed across the sky.

"That's it," she said. "Can you feel it? We're moving faster."

"Is he following us?"

Estra looked back. "That's hard to tell."

"What if he is?"

She didn't answer.

"Tell me," he said.

"He's unpredictable. He eats clouds. He could devour the ship. And you with it."

Arden laughed.

She shuddered, lips trembling. "You're vapor, Arden. Just vapor."

"Ingis eats clouds."

"Ingis lives to feed Ingishead." Estra frowned, facing forward again. "Slower." She turned her head, gauging their progress against the scuds they were passing. "We don't want to draw his attention."

Arden loosened his grip on the rail.

"There are things I haven't told you," Estra said. "Things you need to know. Ingis is a hunter. A killer. The storm is a graveyard—a monument to the fallen."

"It's vapor," Arden said. "It's a cloud."

"But it's taken his nature. It's infused with his fury, his hunger."

Again, Arden felt a twinge of unreasoning fear. As a child, he could see the savagery in a rain god's face.

"I was oblivious at first. Naive." Estra glanced at him. "The memory's indelible—the night I realized what it meant to be a predator."

Suddenly rain was pelting the ship, dimpling the deck, blurring the bulwarks. Arden could feel the heavy drops falling through him, jarring his motes, unsettling them.

Estra looked over her shoulder. "It wasn't yet dark. I was standing in the Eyehole with him, inflamed by the thrill of the chase. Our prey was a small cloud, and there was no one aboard. I didn't think it would bother me.

"Our winds swept it closer. An innocent thing. Unsuspecting, harmless. A pink glow in the west had tinted its billows. I could see it being pulled into Ingishead's neck. Its scarves were shredding, puffs tearing loose. I could hear it being crushed as it entered the Jowls. I could feel its struggles. The Jowls rumbled and shook. As the little cloud's energy joined our own, the Cranium crackled. I looked up and saw Ingishead growing, gaining a few dozen feet."

"To be bigger," Arden said.

Estra nodded. "That's what thunderheads do. They eat other clouds to grow, and to boost their power. Those are the facts of the sky."

"What's the point?"

"The point is More," Estra said. "The glory of More. Storm clouds eat and eat; they get bigger and bigger, more and more powerful. And one day they explode."

Arden looked back. "He's veering to the east. I don't think he's chasing us."

Estra checked. "He may be tacking or riding the trades. We're going west." She faced forward and altered their course. The rain thinned to a drizzle.

"What is that?" Arden pointed.

A wavering belt crossed the sky, the color of butter.

"A heat band," Estra said.

"It's beautiful."

"We stay away from those," she said. "They cut clouds to pieces. Dissolve them to nothing."

"How many years were you with him?"

Estra didn't reply. The silence drew out. Had she heard his question?

Finally she shook her head. "We started on a cloud smaller than this one. Growth seemed important then, to protect ourselves. He'd see a cloud that was larger, and be instantly fearful. And angry—that ours was so lacking. We had spindles—a few. His wishes were warning signs, but I didn't heed them."

As she spoke, her body grew more translucent. She was disclosing things she'd been reluctant to share.

"The growth was innocent at first. We gathered mist, we bumped into scuds and absorbed them. One day, he explained his real ambition. And he began to practice."

"Practice?"

"Being a storm cloud." Estra stared ahead. "I helped.

"I kept telling myself, 'That's big enough—he'll be happy now.' But he never was. Ingis will always be a man on a little

94

cloud, wanting a bigger one; and a man on a big cloud who longs for the little one he lost."

Arden peered at her.

"There's a division in his nature," Estra said. "He wants to be loved. Desperately. The more distance there was between us, the more desperate he got. It hurt him—that I remembered the days when our cloud was smaller."

"That didn't stop him."

"No. His wish was bigger than both of us."

Estra looked aft, avoiding his eyes. "The last year was our worst. He was so . . . dependent."

"On you."

"He needed praise every hour of the day," she said. "His vanity was nothing but a mask for his shame. I helped him exalt himself, but it was an endless task. Nothing can fulfill him. He'll never be complete."

"Why did you wait so long to leave?"

"It was—" A painful pause. "The electricity."

Arden watched her.

"When those dazzling swords were crossing the Cranium, and I was shaking with all that power inside me—" Estra's face darkened.

The rumble grew louder, and when Arden turned, the storm seemed closer. Much closer.

"He's gaining—"

As Estra looked back, a following wind battered the ship. Her eyes flared, and her face went white.

There was no question now—Ingis had them in sight.

95

"Bear down," Estra said.

A grooved arcus roiled at the base of Ingishead's neck, pale scuds churning on either side. The swollen head was enormous. For the first time, Arden could see what might have been a face in the forward billows. Not a human face. Its brow was rumpled and its eyeholes were black. Its cheeks were clawed, and there was no mouth or chin.

"Bear down," she cried with a frantic look.

Arden tightened his grip on the rail. "Can we outrun him?"

"Faster, we have to go faster," she said.

"He wants you."

"He thinks he owns me," Estra said. "Nothing has changed. I never should have come back here." The last she said under her breath. She looked at Arden with regret in her eyes. "The time for drifting is over."

Night had fallen and rain lashed the ship. Despite their efforts, it pitched and careened. Ingishead was gaining quickly now, towering behind them, its winds unremitting. Arden squinted to see through the blast. The monstrous head was lit by silver flashes, and its crown grazed the stars.

Between crashes of thunder, the sound of cranes reached his ears. Estra heard them too. She turned, and they searched the sky together. "There," she pointed.

Arden spotted their flock, a thousand feet above, in a wedge formation. Their pattern was tight—the downswing of each bird's wings embraced the one ahead—and their stutters were frenzied. He could hear their excitement. Ingis was following them.

"They gave us away," Estra said, as if she was blaming herself.

The cranes wheeled in the sky above the bows, then one folded its wings and the others took the cue, diving in sequence, unwinding the string from its circle. They called to each other as their legs swung down; then they backflapped and landed on the foredeck.

Arden's face burned, imagining Ingis had read the words he had penned. For the first time since he'd left the earth, he felt truly alone. Estra seemed hopelessly distant. The storm was roaring behind him, but Arden heard only her silence.

She'd seduced him, warped his instincts with what she knew was a lie. Live for the moment. Create our cranes. Never mind our direction. "The True Destination." He'd believed it all—believed they could drift for the rest of their lives.

His simplicity made him sick.

Danger, vigilance, hatred— Ingis was another overlord, the same enemy that had stalked him all his life.

The storm was right behind them, a decapitated head glaring down from the stars, cheeks furrowed with seeping gashes, crown anvil-edged, its interior flashes fringed with electric nets. The corded neck buckled, and the storm's face descended, its chrome beak gleaming, brow trenched with a murderous rage.

"He's in there?" Arden gazed at Estra.

97

She nodded.

"Where?"

Estra pointed her finger at her left eye.

Arden found the dark orbit below the billowing brow. It was strobing with light. Was Ingis standing there, watching him? For a moment, Arden imagined himself looking out, seeing everything Ingis had seen, the endless vistas, the far-flung places— Ruler, champion—the world's lord and king.

The storm's thunder shook the ship. Webs of electricity crawled over his arms.

"Juice," Estra warned.

A current flickered inside her—a nerve tree that crackled in her belly and lit up the vapor from her hips to her chest. Electric jags sprouted like weeds from her joints, and now they were leaping from her shoulders to his.

Arden grasped her and turned her toward him. The charge flashing inside her grounded. As the current sparked from his hands to his feet, Estra's eyes refocused and her trembling ceased.

But the thunder was mounting again, and so was the current. Wires of light arced between Arden's fingers. He imagined the suffering of Ingishead's victims, their struggles, their vain attempts to escape or resist.

"Toward the herd," Estra shouted, gripping the rail.

Off the starboard bow, Arden saw a herd of cottony clouds, grazing like sheep. He clutched the rail, steering with her. Together they shifted the Prow.

Ingishead glowered. The Eyehole sucked, flashing and

black, flashing and black. A deafening roar, it bulged and turned silver, temples swelling. The anvilled brow tilted, focusing its power; then a glowing wicker webbed the storm's head, a network of jagged threads, hissing and white.

A sword of light emerged from Ingishead's cheek and plunged through the stern, devastating the Lofts. The ship heeled and listed. The winds hurled Arden aside and picked Estra up. He reached for her, grappling with all his strength.

The corded neck swelled like the trunk of an ancient tree, impossibly broad, unthinkably tall. The head boiling atop it mushroomed like the bombs of legend, churning and curling up under itself. Ingishead roared.

"Don't," Estra screamed. Her face was raised to the livid billows. "Don't you dare."

There was rage in her eyes, and her fists were clenched, no longer translucent. They were gray, like hunks of lead.

Ingishead shook the sky, filling it with light, firing another bolt. It struck the foremast, dissolving it in a shower of droplets, and its tattered sheets were borne away by the wind.

"He's brewing another," Estra warned.

Arden could feel the tension.

In the Eyehole, he saw the silhouette of a man, with a glowing web behind him. And—in a flash—a man of vapor, as naked as he.

We're defenseless, Arden thought.

"Cut our speed," Estra shouted, smacking his hands from the rail.

The herd of cottony sheep was before them. They coasted

among the grazing clouds and slowed to a crawl. Arden looked around him. The herd was vast—there were thousands of them. The ghost ship was just another cumulus, drifting along. The cranes were huddled on the foredeck now. He turned to them with a threatening look. One unfolded its wings, as if about to betray him.

"Down, get down," Estra said, dragging him to his knees.

Ingishead rumbled close, rotating slowly, ready to strike. But the man in the Eyehole couldn't pick the ghost ship out of the herd. The sheep were senseless, passive and oblivious as the storm barged through them, swelling and pouring down torrents. Ingishead thundered and struck, and struck again, tearing the hides out of a dozen sheep. But it didn't devour them—it left their carcasses drifting.

"What's happening?" Arden wondered.

"He can't tell which I'm on," Estra whispered.

"So he's not going to eat them."

She put her finger to her lips.

Ingishead's bolts continued to prod the senseless clouds. Finally it roared with scorn and backed away.

Arden and Estra huddled on the Bridge, watching it retreat.

But it didn't go far. As the darkness thickened, Ingis posted himself where he had a view of the herd. The storm's rumbling settled, and its lightning dimmed like a dying head bulb on some toiler's brow.

5

Arden woke in the hammock with his heart racing. The air was cold. His head was damp. In his dream, he and Estra were still driving the ghost ship, fleeing from Ingis. He reached through the darkness and felt for her.

She wasn't there.

The ship's billows huffed in the wind. The rigging was humming. From the hull, somewhere below, came wheezing sounds.

He stood. His neck twitched, and he shivered. The misty drapes were open. In that quarter, the sky was clear, but as Arden listened, he could hear Ingishead grumbling. Close, very close—

His face prickled. As he stumbled forward, a spark arced between his hand and the Band Shell. He looked down—electric twigs were crossing his chest. The ship heaved, and a blast of wind ripped gobbets out of the terrace.

Beyond the Band Shell, an ashen fog mantled the ship from bulwark to bulwark. Its roils were dense, and there was no seeing through them. Was it Ingishead? Was the storm's giant Cranium somewhere above? Was he consuming the ship?

The cranes were gathered on the Bridge, stilted, standing erect; and in their midst was a shadowy figure. Was it Estra?

He hurried forward. The boiling black vapor filled his sight. Somewhere above, charges were crackling, and through the dense whorls, silver lights flashed.

Arden reached the Bridge's lower story, put his arms to his sides and kicked off. He rose to the top of the mount, and as he settled onto it, the cranes turned. He saw fear in their eyes; and then, as one, they raised their stuttering cries, lifting into the air, scattering in all directions. At the same time, the shadowy figure twisted and rose, disappearing into the ashen whorls.

He launched himself into them, reaching his arms, flexing his trunk, trying to follow. Crackling, a flash— He got a glimpse of a hand and a pale leg, and then the whorls were blurring, stretching, leaning— Was Ingishead detaching from the ship?

The air around Arden went dark, and a torrent of rain came down. Through the flood, a moan mounted—not a roar of triumph, but a terrible sound, weak and beggared, ravaged by longing and vexed desire. Private despair, secret relief— Not a sound Arden was meant to hear.

His motes were bristling. His body shook.

Then an enormous blade, silver-blue, stabbed through the darkness, striking his head, blinding him and hurling him down.

When Arden revived, the sky had paled. He was on the Bridge, curled on his side. He raised his head, seeing the ship was intact. And Estra— Had Ingishead sucked her up? Was she with Ingis now? Crazy, he thought. A crazy dream. He closed his eyes and took a deep breath.

As he stood, he saw a white weed on his arm. A lightning pattern covered his front, as if a current had frozen his motes as it raced through him. The branching fronds crossed his hips and wound down his legs. He shook his head, ignoring the sight, and turned, scanning the sky.

The air had cleared around the ship. The herd of cottony clouds was gone. In the distance, off the port bows, was a storm cloud. Rain smeared its footing, but its neck and head were in sharp relief. "That's not Ingis," he said, as if there was someone beside him who needed convincing. The head wasn't windswept, and the neck was pale. Another storm, he thought. It was creeping toward the horizon like an uprooted mushroom.

Arden descended and wandered the bows. The foremast was gone, and its collar was frothing. "Estra?" he called. No sign of her there. He headed back to the ship's waist, circling the Bridge, winding his way through the Spindles. "Estra—"

What was he doing? She'd awoken in the night, he thought. Found a place to hide. "She's here," he said, as if someone was listening.

He checked the Glitter Deck and the Bower, and then the stern. The Lofts were torn up, but the stern was untouched. She was stunned, fearful. Or senseless, asleep— She was here, on the ship.

Near the mizzenmast, he came upon a sinkage, covered over with scarves. When he stripped a few off, a vertical passage appeared. A dark and misshapen well. Strange, he thought. In their time aboard, they had somehow missed this.

"Estra?" Her name echoed in the well. Arden stepped into it and levitated down.

At the bottom, a small space opened around him, the size of his cell in the ziggurat. The air in the chamber was still, and the sounds were muffled.

Its sides were irregular, curved, tapered together above him like a newly pulled onion; and every surface was a fabric of straws—cords of white mist strung together, uneven and loose, like a basket woven by someone who'd never made one before. Estra wasn't here.

Arden touched the surface before him, and his hand burst. All that remained was a nimbus of drifting powder. He waved his stump through it, collecting the motes, reassembling his hand. The Chamber, he saw, had come alive. The basket was flexing, every straw spinning on its long axis, kinking and stiffening, swelling and dwindling along its length. The weave loosened and tightened as the basket flexed; it rumbled and growled like an empty stomach; and then, as if it had found its purpose, the basket began to contract around him.

Arden put his hands to his side and kicked off, rising through the shrinking taper and into the well. By the time he reached the deck, the contraction had ceased. With nothing inside it, the Chamber was still.

Arden rose and scanned the ship. There was only one place left to look.

As he approached the Pond, on its far shore, he saw a silhouette through the fog.

"Is that you?" he said.

The silhouette turned, and then others were visible. The birds stood one-legged, as always, with the mists swirling around them.

"Where is she?" he demanded.

Then he rushed at the cranes, flailing his arms and cursing.

Their silver necks twitched, they thrust their beaks at him, panic in their amber eyes. The birds lifted in a struggling mass, wailing at each other. Then they swooped and plummeted over the gunnels.

He watched them tumble beneath the ship, squawking, unfolding their wings, thrashing, stroking. One aimed itself and began to glide, and others joined the line.

"Don't come back," Arden shouted.

They began to stutter, a mournful chorus with a maudlin note, as if they were taunting him. Arden turned away.

He was alone. Alone in the sky. Frightened and fooling himself.

He headed back to the Bridge.

Estra was gone.

Had Ingis spoken through her dreams? Had she been in some kind of trance? Did he use some kind of threat or coercion? When they collapsed in the hammock together, she'd voiced her fears. This was just the beginning, she said. Arden had tried to be optimistic. At some point, Ingis would realize that she had made her choice. But while he was hoping, Ingis had been plotting to take her back.

Every minute he'd spent searching the ship was a minute lost.

An hour later, Arden was threading a maze of large cumuli. He spotted a channel that looked plowed by Ingis and headed toward it, gripping the rail, focusing, steering. The storm cloud was out of sight now, but there was a trail to follow. He had to make the ship go faster.

Estra's abduction galled him. He was fearful of what might be happening aboard. Had Ingis already forced himself on her? Was he doing that right now? Arden felt the violation in every mote of his being. And with the sense of violation came an increase in speed. His upset, he realized, was adding thrust. Anger, it seemed, increased the wind-churn and upped the cloud's momentum.

For hours, he tormented himself—for being a lamb, for being so green—and he got some acceleration. But there wasn't much to gain. He reached the limit of the ship's power quickly, and after that, his fury was pointless. All he could do was to envy Ingishead's size and speed.

As the sun was setting, the storm came into view again, farther away, moving north and west. With its flashes to guide him, and with the help of the moon and stars, Arden piloted the ship all night, into the dawn and the heat of the following day. And when the next night came, he was still at the helm, bleary and weak. When the third day began, he was nodding in fits, dreaming on his feet. That head, that grisly head— He could see it, black and boiling against a bronzed sky, like a monstrous tree burl; or hanging from the moon's crescent like a mask, with the string of cranes sliding through its Eyehole. Then he and Ingis were face to face; and it was the man, not the cloud, with clawed cheeks, an overhung brow and a missing eye.

I have to sleep, Arden thought.

He scraped together some mist for quilting and a pillow and lay down on the Bridge, hoping he could nap at intervals and still keep his speed and direction. And it worked. His purpose remained keen, and the ship's winds kept churning. He would wake abruptly, fix on the way forward, then sink back down.

As he followed the storm, he saw signs of its passage on the world below—flooded basins and mudslides, lanes in the forests leveled by twisters, heaped trunks and choked rivers. Lightning had struck a hill country and burnt it black. The fire's smoke made the sky hazy, then Ingishead cleared it with rain. The storm slowed, and the ghost ship closed much of the distance.

With only a screen of mist between them, Arden watched Ingishead drown the land. Leaden streaks slanted beneath its thundering crown. "A rain god," he said wryly, imagining Ingis and Estra at the Eyehole together. Ingis had his arms spread, playing the great irrigator. "Look what I do."

An hour later, the storm passed over a settlement, billows churning, livid above and ashen below. The sweeping neck lowered a funnel that razed the frightened valley, tearing up buildings, sucking bodies and rubble into it.

The sights sobered Arden. As close as he was to the storm now, he was asking himself what he intended to do if he caught up to it. Or if Ingis spotted him.

Ingishead was eating every cloud in its path.

A cirrus that looked like a comet with a flowing tail—the finest white fibers all stranded together. It must have heard the storm behind it, but it seemed not to care. Easy pickings for Ingis.

Near the sky's ceiling, a cloud hung motionless, fronted with tangled ringlets, like a hermit peering out of a cave. As Ingis approached, the hermit shook his head, but there was no weather in him, and no electricity. Winds from Ingishead grabbed him and dragged him down. Where the Cranium met the cockled neck, the cloud was torn to pieces.

A stratus with a rippling back rafted low in the sky, like a sluggish creature sunning in a swamp. It was soft and compliant, and the thunderhead engulfed it without a fight.

Radiant, dingy, fibrous or plump—Ingis didn't care. He hunted them all. When it fixed on prey, the storm's face trenched and its anvil sharpened, driving through heaven like a doomsday ark. Frozen or chased, the preys' fate was the same. Ingishead overcame them, digesting them in its rumbling Jowls. Then a moment later, the Cranium crackled and swelled, and its power spiked.

Why hadn't Ingis devoured the ship? Why hadn't Ingis eaten him? Was the ship so small? Did Arden mean so little? Ingis had Estra now—what did he care?

Arden trailed Ingis across two snow-capped ranges and a bony gorge, hiding behind mists and fog banks and hurrying forward. Ingis kept to his heading, north and west, pausing only to feed, ravage the earth and fill the heavens with roaring. How big could Ingishead be? That needed some imagination.

North and west, north and west. Arden shook himself from sleep to find it was already dawn. He'd lost control of the ship, he thought. But when he stood, he saw that it was still on course, still moving at high speed. And when he put his hands on the rail, a strange calm crept up his arms, as if the ship meant to reassure him. Did it want what he wanted, could it feel what he felt? He discovered that he could be absent from the Bridge for long stretches. It seemed that the ship had somehow absorbed his purpose, and was now a part of him. Was it because he was so alone?

Ingishead reached a great river delta. It floated over the water with hardly a rumble, the sky gray and empty around it. Was Estra thinking of him? Was she as lonely as he was?

Arden missed her desperately.

They spoke to each other in the hammock. Once he dropped off, he'd hear her voice in his ear. And he would find himself mumbling to her as he surfaced from sleep. But his waking hours were anguished. She'd freed herself, cast herself loose of Ingishead, he thought, imagining she was floating in the fog nearby. His cranes had come to their senses and borne her away, he thought. They'd descended on Ingishead, loaded her into a net of mist and made their escape. Fantasies.

He did his best to fight off dark thoughts, but they plagued him throughout the day. What had Ingis done to her? Where was he taking her? Arden feared he would never get her back. He would spend the rest of his life following Ingis, more lonely than he'd been on earth.

Estra, he thought. My soul, my joy, my never-setting sun. The words to describe how I'm feeling— They're trapped in my heart. They echo there, crying to be heard. When you're with me again— I won't speak them till then.

At day's end, he left the Bridge and made his way to the Lofts, hoping he'd find some peace there. The lightning strike had ripped through the hillocks, leaving a narrow canyon; but wafting vapor had filled the gap, and winds were smoothing its ragged edges. Arden sank into a mound of oakum, imagining Estra beside him, resting her cheek on her hand. "Be patient," he said. "Somehow I'll get you back." Then he was curling in Mariod's arms, filling her ears with a child's woe.

The next morning, as he rose to the Bridge, he saw the cranes had returned. They were standing on the foredeck, words of love still scribed on their wings. When they saw him, they raised a stuttering chorus.

They've been following me, he thought. Their voices seemed meddling and piteous, and their urgency seemed to mock him. Were they buddying up just to hector him? Did they enjoy his suffering? Maybe they wanted him to return to the Pond, to produce more of their worthless kind.

He was wrung out, disheartened by no one and nothing but himself. Ingis had stolen his love, and here he was, tagging behind them in a powerless scud. His incapacity disgusted him. When he'd left the earth, he had imagined he was finally escaping that.

With an irony bitter and bleak, Arden opened his arms to Ingis.

"Who could challenge the one and only?" he said. "Almighty. Destroyer. The infinite I-N-G.

"Ingis— There is no god like you, and there never will be. For those with hope, you're just a vile projection. For toilers like me, you're the truth—the Supreme Commander."

His future had departed, leaving only the past.

"Arden the brave," he snarled. "Arden the free."

He raised his fists and shook them.

The air turned colder. The winds blew more fiercely. The hours of daylight shrank. It was clear Ingis wasn't wandering. His direction was constant—north and west. On the earth below, slid a puzzle of white and dark pieces; then the dark pieces fell out.

Ingishead was advancing toward the pole. The great mushroom cap was releasing white spores now, blanketing everything with snow. Trying to keep a safe distance, using mists for cover, Arden followed the storm across a frozen sea. There were gaps in the ice cakes; then Ingishead sealed the gaps, and Arden couldn't tell whether there was sea or land below. All was white and level, barren and bearingless.

His breath fogged the air. The deck glittered with spicules, the rails of the Bridge were cased in ice. He imagined Estra was standing beside him, keeping him warm, her lips by his ear. He could hear her whispering, "You pilot for two." The cranes seemed not to notice the cold. They huddled on the foredeck while it snowed, and at the end of each day, they descended to the iced-over Pond, where they spent the night. Arden curled in the hammock, manning the helm while he slept, his torpid motes squealing and creaking. The winds cracked the torn sheets and the Mainmast groaned. How cold could it get?

The next morning dawned clear. The snowing had ceased, and the oblique rays of the sun glazed Ingishead's front. The storm cloud was slowing.

Arden steered the ship behind a cloud bank, pressing forward. Through the cloud bank's comber, he could see the thunderhead looming closer. Then, all at once, an icy fog rose. In seconds, the view disappeared. The sky vanished and so did Ingishead.

Arden let go of the rail and halted the ship. The fog was so thick, he couldn't see the Bridge. A wheeze reached him from below, muffled, distant.

He descended to the deck. The gunnels were bristling with hoar. He moved along them, looking for a break. There was none. The whiteout had engulfed the ship.

Arden posted himself at the Prow, hoping the air would clear, hoping the currents wouldn't carry him under the nose of Ingis. Hours later, he was still standing there, senses fogged. Concentration was useless. There was no object now, no trail; he couldn't drive blindly forward.

He put his hands over his eyes. Where was he? Where was he really? When he removed his hands, the fog would be gone. He would see, he would know— But when he lowered his hands, the fog was still there.

"You must be freezing," he whispered, as if Estra could hear him.

He reached out to touch her cheek. Was she still lucid? Was she as hazy as he was? She's not here, he thought. And neither was the ghost ship. Or Ingis and the polar barrens. Nothing remained outside of himself. A few memories of the pleasures of earth were still there. Eating a pear cake, whittling a pencil— The sound of a cricket's chirp echoed in the void, thrilling and poignant. The earth, with all its grit, its hard-edged sensations—

The memories were fleeting, fading—vestiges of a vanished world. His legs were numb now, and the numbness was moving up his arms. What could sustain him? He was losing everything, even his own intangible body.

He swept his arms through the fog. White, white—Nothing but white. Don't panic, he thought. Then he lost what sensation remained in his arms. He couldn't tell whether the ghost ship was moving or not. He was sightless, freezing, suspended in space. Drifting toward Ingis, for all he knew.

Arden turned and stumbled his way back along the gunnels till he reached the Bower. He sank to the terrace and crawled across it, feeling his way toward the Band Shell, finding, at last, the comfort he sought beneath the hammock. He curled there, muttering to himself, full sentences at first, then phrases and fragments, losing connectives to the cold. People and objects went next, along with any hint of future or past; until his rambling was nothing but a stream of rhymes ending in I-N-G. It was speech from a realm where nothing was complete. Everything was growing, becoming.

He crossed the borderline of dream, and continued reeling off gerunds in his sleep.

Sun flashed on the icicles fringing the Band Shell. Arden found himself huddled beneath the hammock, crusted with rime. His limbs were still numb, but the mist was clearing around him.

He came to his feet, crossed the terrace and parted the drapes, the sparkling fabric slinking through his fingers.

Above, stretched an endless sky. Beneath, perpetual ice.

The ghost ship was over an arctic plain, pocked with craters and seamed with faults. Where was Ingishead? Arden scanned the polar expanse, catching sight of a line of prints. Two white bears were lumbering over the snows, headed for the dawn glow. As he watched, the bears' backs flamed. The sun edged higher, the snow around them flared, and they were lost to view.

When he faced forward, he could see the cloud bank. He was still in its lee. Towering into the sky above it, was the Cranium of Ingishead.

Arden rose to the Bridge. Sensation was returning to his hands. He gripped the rail, braced himself, focusing on Ingishead, and eased the ship forward, feeling fresh confidence. There was a following wind, and when he halted the ship at the end of the cloud bank, the wind muzzed the bows, veiling the Prow.

The sun had edged above the horizon. The sky was magenta, and the ice was gold; and in the space between the ghost ship and Ingishead, a thousand pink snakes were coiling up.

Where are you? Arden mouthed the words, his breath fogging the air.

The storm cloud hovered over a plateau webbed with cracks. There were pools all around it; and on the shores of the pools, Arden saw cranes. The quiet was pierced by stuttering cries, and a large flock appeared, circling the Cranium. The formation dove, descending to the pools and settling among them. Arden looked over his shoulder. His birds were still roosting at the Pond. Surely they could hear their cousins.

Something shifted in the Eyehole, catching the light.

When Arden looked up, every mote in his body jittered. Estra was standing in the Eyehole, looking out. She was alone, a phantom draped in flowing scarves. She wrapped her arms around herself, feeling the cold.

It was hard to tell, she was at such a great height— But she didn't look injured. Was she caged or leashed in a chamber up there? Was she still in shock? The way she held herself, she looked distressed. Miserable. Forlorn. As hopeless as he had been. If she only knew how close he was.

She looked regal up there. The magnificence of the storm cloud suited her. But not the locale. Ingis had taken her to the end of the earth.

Estra stepped back inside, and the Eyehole was blind again.

When the sun set, Arden knelt on the Bridge, mentally braced. He reviewed his plan once and again, waiting for midnight. Exhaustion intruded, and his thoughts drifted. He brought them back and was starting through the plan again when he fell asleep.

He dreamt of the two bears. He was one of them, and the other was Ingis.

In his dream, the ghost ship had turned keel up. It was a white mountain, with an icy crest. At its base, a rumpled carpet was spread, and the two bears were sleeping on it. Ingis breathed deeply, the wind chugging in his giant muzzle. He stirred and grumbled, reaching for Arden. The fur on his arms was thick and white. The moon rose beneath them. Ingis took hold of Arden in the dim light.

Dry powder flowed in currents around them. White smoke filled the air. Arden was bleary, but he could feel the strength of Ingis. He put a heavy paw on Ingis' shoulder and combed the fur with his claws. It was warm and silky. Arden grabbed bunches of it. Ingis' shoulders tensed, and his massive arms pulled Arden down. Arden buried his brow in the fur on Ingis' chest. The loose powder was drowning them. The mountain was turning onto its side. Arden's thick legs jerked, punching holes in the carpet of cloud. The moon's rays beamed through the gaps, fanning around them like great spans of quartz, bloodless, translucent.

Ingis raised his head into the crossing beams. His white jaws parted, and he began to roar. Arden lifted his muzzle, dazzled, and touched his brother's. And they roared together until they were blind and deaf.

Hours past midnight, Arden woke. The pallid gold of an arctic aurora made the night mists shimmer. He stood, gripped the rail, fixed his eye and his mind on Ingishead's neck, and moved the ship forward. All the lights in the Cranium were off.

He was hundreds of feet in the air, levitating up the corded neck, arms at his sides, legs straight. Below him, the cranes of Ingis were roosting in the pools. They had seen the ship approach; they'd watched him climb into the air, and they were still watching him.

Ingishead's neck was a hanging slaughterhouse, its cockles leaden and oily, strung with thick ropes of fog, like veins or ligaments. As Arden rose, the winds grew stronger, blasting him against the grooves of the neck. The ropes were icy, and when he grabbed them, he found he could use them to boost himself up. Sucking sounds echoed inside the neck. As he passed a lesion, he could see the black tunnel and feel the rush of air within.

Would Ingis sleep soundly? How much time did he have, Arden thought, before Ingis woke? The quiet persisted as he drew closer to the Cranium's underside. He could feel its charge. His limbs had been tingling when he left the ship, and the tingle had spread to his chest as he rose. Now every mote of his body was buzzing. Winds circled the giant head. They were biting cold, and they increased as he approached, lifting peels of vapor, raising boils on boils.

The Cranium was much larger than Arden had imagined. Suspended in space, a planet of its own— A grave rumble sounded inside it. He prayed Ingis wouldn't stir. Above, the neck joined the monstrous head. He planted his soles on an icy cord, flexed both legs and kicked, driving himself away from the neck. Then he was climbing through the winds that circled the storm's head.

Higher, still higher, fighting to keep himself stable—

Below the Eyehole, he spotted a gash in Ingishead's cheek,

swirling with mist. Arden extended both arms, drew one knee up and arrowed through it.

The Cranium's cold struck him, but even as he shivered, his hopes rose. He sculled his arms and lowered his feet to the quilting. I'm here, he thought.

Along with the buzzing charge, he felt the prick of drifting needles. Ice spicules bit his nose and stuck like pins in his throat. The air was murky, but after a moment the space around him resolved. He was in a cloistered maze, lit by electric flickers and crossed with shadows. He stepped forward, listening, peering ahead. A ribbed passage was lit. He moved along it. The auroral glow glimmered through its lancets.

As the passage turned, the Cranium's interior came into view. An icy breath choked him. He covered his mouth with his hand. Through veils of fog, he could see the great walls curving up. The ceiling was ribbed, and the ribs swelled as he watched, and so did the billows between. They churned and shifted, revealing glimpses of the night and stars—fleeting transoms that connected in strange patterns, appearing and pinching to nothing.

Spirals of fog crossed the space, crackling and flashing as their charges diffused, descending as embers with prismatic halos. The electricity of Ingis surrounded him: an invisible web. Arden struggled to imagine what it would be like when Ingis was awake and the power was peaking.

A chorus of warbling moans reached Arden's ears, and as he watched, a flock of white creatures sailed through the

Cranium. Headless, like triangle kites with long tails, the creatures banked blindly in the crackling space, veering into half-domes and cupolas, where they moaned and banged and hung themselves like empty garments.

Arden scanned the walls lower down. Mist nets and mist webs. Festoons of frost, dripping stalactites. The dome's struts were twisting, blooming at their tops; and the vaults between were crawling with foggy embossings—frescoes that changed, moment by moment. Lightning fantasies, merciless strokes, attacks and gorgings; the rapture of growth and the frenzy of feeding— Arden turned, seeing and feeling. It was here the glories of More were enshrined.

Each fresco was lit by sparking bursts and spiderous feelers. Each arched and boiled as Arden watched, envisioning some still greater atrocity, while crusts of ice and inlaid frost shattered loose and hissed down the walls.

Bridges and catwalks spanned the vaults. Arden imagined Ingis here, reveling in his conquests. Below the frescos, above the open arcades, a skirt circled the dome. On it, was a living inscription. The stylized letters crawled like worms: *King of Heaven, Beholden to None.*

Suddenly the electric fog in the Cranium's center was washed with color. The embers fizzed and their halos expanded, connecting and blending into each other. Coral lips, fifty feet wide. Arched brows and a high forehead. The familiar edge of her nose— Pieces of Estra infused the fog. The veils and scarves were weaving together; and as they did, the glittering fabric became three-dimensional, as real as life.

Arden saw the emotion in Estra's eyes. What is this? he wondered. It was an image of a woman in love. And there were sounds to match, sighs of longing and fulfilled desire.

Her face receded and was joined to a body. A memory, Arden thought. A wish for the future. Then a second creature appeared below Estra—a kneeling man, humbling himself. Was that Ingis?

Estra looked down, eyeing the man with contempt, refusing to touch him. And as the man begged, his body shriveled and his neck lengthened. Claw marks appeared on his face. One eye dissolved, and his nose turned into a beak. The more Estra spurned him, the more monstrous he got.

Ingis is dreaming, Arden thought.

No longer a shrine to gratified hunger, the Cranium was a theater now, playing a tragedy. Even as he slept, Ingis knew: he could steal Estra back, he could hold her against her will, but he couldn't force her affections. And with all his power, he couldn't turn the tragedy off.

A phantom rumbling echoed in the Cranium. As Arden watched, the suspended Estra reshaped and darkened, turning into a storm. Instead of being predator, Ingis was prey; and the cloud bearing down on him was Estra.

Arden turned, scanning the lower cloisters. Through an archway hung with veils, he saw a giant circle of night, like a rosette window. He hurried across the cushioned floor. On either side of the arch, cranes were stilted. An urn crackled and smoked, electric thistles flashing from its mouth. When Arden stepped through, he was in a roomy chamber, with the

Eyehole before him; at the rear, Estra was asleep on a bed large enough for a gang of toilers.

She lay prostrate, twisted in a gown of fog. The bed was strewn with silks and translucent fabrics. The boudoir was gloomy, palatial but freezing. Estra wasn't bound, but as he approached, he felt the buzz increasing, and he wondered if she was caged in some kind of electric field.

Her gown was sequined with ice. When he stooped over her, he could smell an exotic perfume. Arden froze, unexplainably fearful. So much had changed. Would she be the same when he woke her?

"Estra." He touched her back.

There was frost on her lashes. He grasped her shoulder and shook her. "Estra—"

One arm stirred. She turned onto her hip. Her face looked leaden. He gazed at her arms and her thigh, afraid he'd see burns or cuts, signs of a struggle.

Estra's eyes opened. At the sight of him, they were disbelieving.

Her cheek was slick. A drop fell from her chin.

"Where is he?" Arden asked.

She shivered. "In the Jowls, I guess. How did you get here?"

"You're all that matters to me." He slid his arms beneath her and lifted her up.

Her gaze fell on his sternum and the lightning scars.

"He struck me the night he carried you off," Arden said.

Estra cringed and closed her eyes.

Their bodies touched, and his chest sparked. He could

smell through her perfume now—an acrid odor, like fumes of ignition. How many times—and where—had Ingis abused her? Borne away, with lightning and thunder, freezing cold and the furious winds—

"I didn't think I'd ever see you again," she said.

Her eyes were shut. He could feel the tension in her limbs and frame.

Then she drew a breath and looked at him, her eyes deepening, seeing the long journey he'd taken and the risks he'd run. Her features softened. She embraced him and held him tightly. They kissed, and the breath that escaped their lips emerged in wisps. The ice on her lashes was melting. A tear fell on her cheek.

"He was cruel to you," Arden said.

She shook her head, as if refusing to burden him.

He set her down, turning her toward the Eyehole. "We're getting out of here."

Estra was still shaking her head. "You deserve better."

Her words surprised him. Was it modesty speaking?

Estra faced the arctic night. "It's freezing out there."

He looked down. The ghost ship was far below. The Cranium's rumbling was faint. Ingis was still asleep. "Now," Arden said, his hand on her back.

She stepped to the Eyehole's rim. When he drew beside her, she spread her arms and threw herself out. Arden followed, and they plunged together, tumbling head over heels. Then she straightened her body, turning head-down. Arden did the same.

A throng of stutters sounded below. The cranes of Ingis were taking wing. They rose as one, forming a V, starting around the storm cloud's neck. They squalled as they spiraled up it, as if they were convinced the threat was real now and were trying to wake him.

The cockles and furrows rushed past; the cracked plateau came closer and closer, the ship grew larger and larger. Estra and Arden sculled and slowed, righting themselves, landing together on the icy Bridge. They turned, put their hands on the rail and got the winds going, steering it away from Ingishead as rapidly as they could.

All the lights in the Cranium came on at once.

The surge of power shook Arden. Over his shoulder, the Cranium was glowing like a giant head bulb. Ingis stood in the Eyehole—naked, arm raised, pointing his finger at him—while the roaring mounted and the sheet lightning flashed behind.

"See how you like it," Arden muttered. "Your dream is real."

He joined his intention to Estra's, and they drove the ship forward.

"Our chances aren't good," she said.

The perpetual snows slid beneath them. The cold teeth of the wind bit Arden's nape. When he looked again, the Eyehole was vacant. Winds were shrieking around Ingishead, circling faster. The storm was moving, its thunder deafening the night, its charge dazzling the sky and the arctic waste. Cranes in her-ringbones flew beside, the flashing light catching their wings.

A ripping sound, and a great sword descended, driving between the starboard bows and the cloud bank nearby.

"He's going to hit us," Estra said.

Arden's limbs trembled. Sparks spit from his fingers.

The great stalk leaned. The Cranium loomed over them. The silver herringbones dragged, trying to keep up.

All at once, the way forward went gray. Arden laughed, straight-arming the rail as the Prow clove through the dense fog of the whiteout.

Another horrific *rip*. The ship shook, and a bolt lit the fog off their stern. And then— They were lost in it, hidden completely.

6

It was daylight. The whiteout was behind them. Aided by a strong tailwind, the ghost ship was moving quickly, the arctic plain gliding beneath it. Arden removed his hands from the rail and turned, checking in all directions. There was no sign of Ingis.

When he returned to the Bower, he found Estra awake in the hammock. She was chalk-white and shivering. A shroud of fog covered her middle. Her shoulders were powdered with ice.

As he stooped over her, she tried to smile.

"You slept." He touched her cheek.

Her forehead creased. "Is he—"

"No. We're on our own now."

"You've left the helm," she said.

"I can do that now. The ship knows me."

Estra looked troubled. "When did this start?"

"Before I crossed the frozen sea."

She peered at the terrace and the Lofts aft, as if seeing the ship with new eyes. "Where are we headed?"

"South."

Arden studied her. "He hurt you."

She quivered and stood, brushing the snow from her shoulders. Then she crossed the Bower, halted at the gunnels and parted the veils, looking down at the polar barrens. She seemed confused, distracted.

Give her time, Arden thought. He moved to join her.

"He's calmer here than he is farther south. He favors the place. He knows I abhor it." She cocked her head, listening.

Arden listened too. It might have been thunder. The sound was so far away, it was like holding a shell to your ear.

"He has cranes of his own," he said.

She nodded slowly. "They roost in the arcades when he's on the move."

"You're glad to be back?"

"Oh yes," she murmured. "So glad, so glad."

"We belong to each other," he said. "To no one and nothing else."

Estra didn't touch him or look at him. She seemed to be sinking into herself. He'd never seen her so withdrawn.

What had happened on Ingishead? he wondered. Did she blame him, that he hadn't been able to protect her? He thought of the long days and nights alone. The memories were dark, and they crowded the space between them. Arden had so many questions— Maybe he shouldn't ask them. Just—put them out of his mind.

Estra took his hand. "We were meant to know love in small pieces," she said. "One at a time. Not all at once."

Her words puzzled him.

They stood in silence. Then she started forward, leading him across the terrace.

"He was going to kill me. That's what he said. He was that angry. And the anger was inward too. He hates himself. Hates that he's allowed the great Ingis to become so dependent."

She took a breath. "I didn't hear Ingishead approach. I was half asleep. Suddenly I could feel its electricity. I was frightened. I got up and— I could see it, settling onto the ship."

"I thought it was going to swallow us," Arden said.

"I went to the Bridge—to talk to him. To reason with him."

"The winds grabbed you," Arden said. He was burning inside, but cautious too. He waited for Estra to speak.

They passed the Mainmast. Between the Bridge and the bows, a new place had arisen, fashioned from hoar by the arctic winds. It was like a garden, a hanging garden, bounded on three sides and open in front. Its icy trellises were thick with leaves of frost and crystalline tendrils that trailed to the deck and over the bulwarks, dragging through the sky.

A snowy bolster had mounded inside the enclosure.

"Let's sit here," she said.

She lowered herself, and he sat beside her.

Was she hiding her pain? Had the abuse from Ingis toughened her?

"What did he do to you?" Arden asked.

"He threatened me."

"He forced himself on you."

She shook her head.

"Taking you to the pole— That's as good as a prison."

She eyed the trellis behind him. "I want to be honest with you."

"About Ingis."

She nodded.

"I had feelings for him once," Estra said. "Strong feelings."

She was avoiding his gaze.

"You were in love," Arden said.

"The first night I spent with you, I put the blame on Ingis. But when I was younger— The life we were leading—" She faced him. "It was a passion we shared. Standing in the Eyehole with Ingishead boiling and all the juice on— I was thrilled by power, and the excitement of Ingishead's growth. You were in the Cranium. Maybe you felt some of its magic. When I was younger— I loved the thundering, and the rush when the bolts reached out." She touched the scar on her breast.

"I understand," he said.

"What Ingis has become—it's as much my fault as his. I was frightened, I felt guilty, but— I wanted Ingishead to grow, as much as he did.

"In the early years, we told ourselves it was all for the good. We made the earth fruitful. Crops needed rain. The forests and fields, the rivers and lakes— The storming of Ingis was a blessing, a boon to mankind. Every land we passed over received the gift of our showers. That justified eating every cloud in sight.

"The larger Ingishead grew, the harder it was to lie to ourselves. Our rain fed the fields, but our hail destroyed them. We drowned the land. We washed forests and cities away. Our fires burnt everything in their path.

"Finally, the mask came off. All our good deeds were just rationalizations for savagery. 'Ingis the Green,' was a sham."

Arden put his hand on hers. "You didn't know who he was."

Silence.

"It's not as simple as that," Estra said. "There were parts of his nature I knew better than he did. He isn't like you. He had people—a family. But his mother ignored him, and his father was heartless—he didn't think his son would amount to anything. The day I met Ingis, I could see the wounded child inside him. He'd given up on love."

"It was pity that drew you," Arden said.

"No. Not pity. What I felt was deeper than that. He had a noble spirit. A wizard's mind. And a striking face. Every angle was sharp, and his eyes were blue. His locks were perfectly black back then. I wove them with silver thread. He spoke with eloquence, but gently. It was a child's voice, full of a child's wonder. The things he said—" She shook her head.

Silence.

"He was a writer," Estra said. "A poet. His words gave life to cranes."

Arden stared at her.

"He hasn't written anything in years, but the birds are still with him. They follow him everywhere. They'll never leave.

"They brought us together. That's how we met. I saw them circling a mountaintop. I climbed to the summit and there he was, writing on the mist of a lake. We talked while he wrote."

Arden was dumbstruck.

Estra turned away. "I'm sorry."

The shadows of the frost leaves twitched on her shoulders. That's why the cranes they'd created at the Pond had betrayed him, Arden thought. Ingis was the source of the feelings Estra had given voice to.

"You hid all of this from me," he said.

"Yes, I did."

"You wanted Ingis the poet back," Arden said.

"I loved making cranes. I wanted to do it with you."

"You led Ingis into the sky?"

"We discovered the Tunnels together. He was desperate to leave."

A chill wind blew through the trellises. The vines unraveled like yarn.

"I have more to confess," she said.

Estra seemed to be changing before his eyes.

"On the Bridge that night," she said, "my old feelings came back. His words were tender. They touched me. He had a soul once. A beautiful soul." She pursed her lips. "I asked him to leave us alone. 'It's over,' I said. But— He was in terrible pain. And the things he told me—"

She took a breath. "I levitated up the neck. I went with him voluntarily."

Her words pierced Arden as if he was flesh again.

She raised her hand, shielding her face. The wind carried ice, diamond dust that glittered and stung, winking and burning as it passed through him.

"What did he say?" Arden asked.

"Things he knew I wanted to hear. Things he knew I didn't."

"Tell me."

"He said he needed my strength, that he couldn't live without it. He spoke of his end with relish, with pleasure. He pleaded—" She stopped herself. "I'm not going to do this."

"You called him a monster."

"There's another side to Ingis," she said. "He swears at the cranes, but whenever he stops, Ingishead drizzles so they have ponds to settle in. And when they're asleep, he walks among them, listening to them purr, making sure they're at peace."

"Why didn't you tell me?"

"I should have. I wanted to."

Estra rose from the bolster and circled the trellis wall, facing aft. Arden stood, following, stopping a few feet behind her. The landscape below the ship was still barren and white.

"Why did you come back with me?" he said.

She gazed at the Bridge, as if remembering that night. "'I still love him,' I thought. But I was wrong. I didn't. Once I was in the Cranium, I realized that. His welcoming kiss— He sealed his lips over mine, and in one inhale, he drew the breath from my lungs. Nothing has changed. He cares about power and getting bigger. I begged him not to take me to the pole, but he wouldn't listen. And he was feeding all the way."

133

"I saw," Arden said.

She closed her eyes. "I didn't want to be that helpless—ever again.

"On the third day, I stood by the Eyehole, imagining where you were and what you were thinking. I was going to jump. 'I'll find my way back somehow,' I thought. And then—I gave up. 'It's too late now. This is your fate. You're not worthy of Arden.'"

She faced him. "That first night— Your dream of love. You said you'd honor my spirit. I knew, I knew."

Arden stood at the Pond's edge, seeing himself on the mirrored surface. Had his face changed? He looked different. He pinched his chin and peered into his eyes.

When Estra suggested the Pond, he'd refused. "Please," she said. "For us." He relented, and she led the way past the Mainmast and down the slope. As they approached, the cranes appeared, lining the far shore. They stuttered and peered at each other discontentedly, as if they too were thinking of Ingis.

She put her hand on his shoulder. "Sit down."

Arden lowered himself onto the rime-covered pallet. Estra knelt beside him.

She extended her arm and swept a skim of the loose powder over the ice.

"The subject?" he said.

"Your courage. The rescue of Estra."

She took his forefinger and guided it onto the page. Then she put her lips to his ear and began to whisper.

Arden's hand moved, making slow figures. Words, more words— His finger followed her dictation, but his mind lagged behind.

"Concentrate," she said gently.

She started whispering again, and his finger moved. But the words still eluded his mind. He could hear their rhythm and texture, picture the shifting of lips and tongue. But what she was saying meant nothing.

A gust grazed the sheet, sifting the powder. Stutters sounded across the water. The cranes batted their wings, lifting into the air. They could tell there was trouble.

"Please," Estra begged him. "Listen to what I'm saying."

Arden nodded, trying to soften his heart.

Estra began again, pouring everything into it.

His finger moved. Her emotion was real. She's still bound to me, he thought.

He continued to scribe, doing his best to feel their kinship. When the page was finished, she lifted it from the surface, and a new crane spread its wings.

But it couldn't fly. It fell to the bank, elbowed its way up the shore and raised itself on quivering legs. The crane eyed them with distrust and hobbled around the Pond's rim, injured or lame. It had an odd voice, half croak, half whimper.

"The genius and his muse," Arden said wryly. He regarded Estra. "Did you think I'd enjoy being a double for Ingis? I've been in servitude all my life."

She bowed her head.

"I hate him," he said. "That's what's on my mind—all the things I'd like to do to Ingis." He motioned at the Pond. "Shall I put that in writing?"

Estra swept a fresh skim of powder across the Pond. "Go ahead. Do you want me to help?"

"Just admire my work," he replied.

With that, he gave vent to his anger, heaping scorn on Ingis, contriving a half-dozen unlikely ways to avenge himself.

When he was done, he sat back. Estra lifted the page.

The bird was shrunken and deformed. It could neither fly nor stand, paddling helplessly on the Pond's ice as the two of them watched.

For Arden, that was enough. But Estra persuaded him to continue. They worked on another page and another. Every sheet added a crane to the flock, each with a new defect. In a couple of hours, the shore of the Pond was littered with broken creatures. Some squawked, some bore their afflictions in silence. One remained standing a few feet from Arden, regarding its reflection as if it was some other bird.

"There's no point to this," he said finally.

"Look at me," Estra said.

He faced her.

"Don't give up on us," she said.

"Listen to you." His sarcasm was thick.

"I'm doing my best—" she said.

"These birds are pathetic."

"All creatures have flaws," she said. "It's your eye that's harsh."

Arden laughed and stood. "I'm seeing them for what they really are."

"What are they—really?" Estra rose.

"Helpless. Sensitive. Weak."

A cold eddy circled them.

"How could you do that to me," Arden said.

Estra didn't answer.

"'Old feelings,'" he snarled, "'strong feelings.' Your secret heart."

Her lips were trembling.

"And his eyes were blue! Lies," Arden raged at her. "Why, Estra? Why?"

She looked away. "There were moments when—"

"What?"

"When I felt something was missing."

He shook his head. "Missing?"

All at once, the memories connected. A hesitation. A sudden eclipse. Estra—distracted, impatient, restless. Her mind was wandering. She was thinking of Ingis.

"What was it you missed?"

Estra was silent.

"What?" he said.

She was alone with whatever her secret self craved.

"I want to know." He spoke so softly, the wind carried his words away.

"The explosion," she said. "The surrender. Being over-come." The last she said with contempt, her eyes full of remorse.

His virgin fantasies, Arden thought. Estra, pleading with Ingis for mercy. Estra, bound and gagged in some murky recess.

"He was the demon in my dreams," she said. "Baiting me, whispering in my ear. 'Fool the fool, but don't think you fool Ingis. The toiler's not for you.'"

"He was with us," Arden said, "the whole time."

"No—"

"It was all a lie."

"Arden, my love for you was real. I swear. They were only moments. Moments of weakness, moments of doubt. Weren't there times that you wondered?"

He shook his head. "Not one."

The demon in Estra's dream was right, Arden thought. He'd been a fool. The perfect union he'd felt with Estra wasn't perfect at all. No matter how much you love someone, you can't know what they're thinking.

"Ingis never had your self-confidence," she said, "or your authenticity. He wasn't your equal when he was younger, and he isn't now. I knew that the night we met. Are you listening to me?"

"Don't waste your fawning on me," he said. "I'm choking with lies. Sick of them. Take them back to Ingis—you deserve each other." His rage had an outlet now. "I'm going to idle the ship. Wait for him. I'll hand you over myself. Will he let me watch? I'd like to see him give you his worst."

She covered her heart with her hands. "Do you want to kill me? Maybe you should."

Arden ran his eyes over her vaporous body, as if weighing how he might do it.

"I never stopped loving you," Estra said. "I lost my way, I let Ingis reach me. But I never stopped." She turned back to the Pond. "We need hope. Hope for the future. Our future. Together." She reached for Arden's hand.

He yanked it back.

"I have the words," she nodded. "They're here inside me." She lowered herself onto the pallet. "I'm not giving up."

Arden turned to leave.

"Hate me," she said, "but don't go. I beg you."

He halted, watching her curry a fresh skim of powder over the surface.

"These words are for you," she whispered. And she lowered her finger.

Here—in this feebling cold, at this cheerless moment, in this desolate place—even here, the dream endures. The dream we share. A dream of harmony, of devotion and wisdom. Are we lost in a wasteland? Locked in the ice? No. The barrens aren't us.

We're still moving forward. Feeling our way.

Though the journey's a long one, an angel is with us. The angel of faith. And the angel knows—

There's safe harbor in a warmer clime. We'll find it.

Our fate, our love, our life together— That's all that matters.

Estra gazed at Arden. Her eyes were glowing.

"We could use an angel," he conceded.

"She's ready to fly." Estra slid her fingers beneath the page and peeled it off. The pinions divided, and the wide wings spread, and a large crane soared into the air, its razor beak gleaming. An angel it was, elegance in silver.

The bird wheeled, climbing the invisible winds, circling over them. Arden followed it, feeling an access of hope amid his pain, wanting to believe. Estra was beside him, her arms around his. The crane continued to rise, fading into a blanket of fog. Its cry reached them like a beneficent prayer.

"We'll find a way," Estra said. "Won't we."

He could feel a spot of sun warming his shoulder. "In my heart, I'm still holding on to you. I don't think I can ever let go."

She touched his lip. He faced her, and she pressed hers to his.

As they drew apart, he gazed at the malformed cranes. "Are we just going to leave them here?"

"They're ours," Estra said. "What else can we do?"

As they approached the Bower, the wind rose. The ship's sails swelled like amber melon halves, and the pennants were dancing.

They halted together before the hammock.

"I want to be close," Estra said.

Arden regarded her.

She raised her brows. "Please, try."

She lay down in the hammock and clasped his hand. He lay beside her.

Slowly their bodies crept together, motes intermingling. Arden paused, holding back, wary. He tried to ignore them, but his suspicions wouldn't go away. They hadn't spoken about her intimacies with Ingis. But they must have occurred. Would Arden feel the man's presence? Were his motes lingering inside her?

He remembered the nights alone on the ship, when he longed to bring current his pent-up desire; when he imagined that he and Estra might, once again, occupy the same physical space.

Then the images he'd seen in the Cranium returned—Ingis, prostrate with desire, wretched and begging.

His motes retreated from Estra's, unwilling to mingle.

A space opened between them, and the rapture atomic faded from view.

Arden saw the frond of white frost on Estra's breast. He couldn't look in her eyes. An ice devil whirled across the terrace.

"That night," he said. "The night he carried you off. Did you make love?"

Estra shook her head, refusing to answer.

"I want to know."

His voice was low and grave. Why was he doing this?

"You shared your motes with him," Arden said.

Estra was silent.

"Ingis possessed you." His tone was grim.

141

"Not with feeling," she said. "Roughly. Without asking."

"Did he please you?"

Estra was silent.

"Did he?" Arden pressed her.

"In his way."

"What way is that?"

"There was nothing of me," she said. "It was all Ingis."

"And it pleased you," he murmured.

Arden felt humiliation in every mote of his being. Estra's features vanished. All he could see were her borders. She was a shadowless sketch, a line drawing without color or depth.

"I hate that I let him treat me like that," she said.

"You didn't resist."

"No, I didn't." Her voice was hoarse with distress. "I let him—be Ingis. It was like that, the night— That's why I came back to earth, the night we met."

"And it's why you left with him."

"There's a division in my nature," Estra said.

The hope that the angel of faith had brought was gone.

"In the clouds," he said, "grief comes easily."

"We are made of tears," Estra said.

Those were the last words they spoke. They lay on their sides facing each other, but they might have been leagues apart. The wind died. When night finally lowered its glittering drape, the Band Shell went gray. Then a light rain began to fall.

That night, Arden dreamt he was back on earth. Fog had descended on the settlement and all the country around it.

142

Impenetrable fog. The windows and doors of the ziggurat were open, and its cells were empty. The people were gone. They were wandering—each on a journey into the void, companionless, on their own.

The ship was speeding south, the arctic barrens finally behind them. Arden and Estra were on the Bridge, and the sky was veiled with mist. As the vapor parted, a giant yellow belt appeared off their port bows.

"Heat band," Estra barked.

Arden cut sharply to starboard. Behind a scurf of mist, a cliff of cloud poured down, a fierce niagara, so close its droplets spattered their faces. The ship heaved and bucked, fighting the tumbling vapor.

Estra checked the way they had come. Through the lingering fog, she spotted Ingishead. Its quiff was flying, and its temples were winged. The Cranium was quiet.

"Does he see us?" Arden said.

"I don't think so."

"We might pass under the Heat Band."

"We might." Estra faced the Cascades.

Bundles of ropy vapor, twisted and knotted, arched as one, plunging down. Huffs of wind batted their faces and thumped in their ears.

"What are you thinking?" Arden said.

"Can you drive the ship under that curl?"

"Too dangerous," he shook his head.

"We don't have any choice," she said, glancing back.

Through the thinning mist, Ingishead's crown looked dark and dense, almost solid. And the man inside— Was he seething, fretting, glum or resentful?

Arden gripped the rail, turning the Prow. "Be ready to levitate," he said. "This may not work."

"We can't lose the ship," she replied. "Give it everything you have."

Arden headed the ship for the tube of the breaking wave. The wind shrieked, the Prow careened— Everything below the Cascades was lost in the roil.

"To port," Estra cried, "to port—"

The currents tugged at the bows. The ship shuddered. The winds bludgeoned its topsides and tore at its sheets. The Mainmast was twisting. Then the stern heeled, and Arden lost his feet. He went down on both knees, but he kept his mind fixed on the course, and the vessel swung to port.

As he rose, the great curl opened before him, the cataract roared, and the Prow slid under its frothing eave.

"We're in it," she shouted.

The next moment, the Bridge plunged. The Cascades' curl was fringed with tongues, and as Arden looked up, they were grappling toward him. A fierce tug, an undertow took hold of the hull; then the ship rolled, turning full over. Hooking winds, drowning foam— He felt Estra's body bump against his, cold as ice.

144

For a moment, the ship seemed to wallow and calm. The niagara no longer thrashed them. Then abruptly the wind rose, stronger than ever. Thunder shook the air.

"It's Ingis," Estra said.

Huddled together, they peered through the Cascades' curtain. Arden could hear the crackling and see the glowing jags lighting the thunderhead's face. The ship bucked in its slipstream as it barreled closer. Would Ingis see them?

The storm's voltage mounted. A spastic discharge lit the Cranium from inside. Cheeks clawed and riddled, the chrome beak, brow overhanging— Ingishead's neck was a mass of cords and torrents, veins and connectives, dragging beneath.

As the thunderhead passed, its Eyehole swept from side to side.

When Ingis was out of sight, Arden managed to pilot the ship out from under the curl. It was high noon by then. The sky was clear, with a gentle breeze. He and Estra stood by the mangled Band Shell, gazing at the remains of their Bower. The terrace was gouged, the drapes were torn, the divans were in pieces. Through a breach in the gunnels, sunlit scuds were visible, floating beside the hull, amber potatoes in an azure stew.

A croak sounded behind him, and when Arden turned, he saw the malformed cranes crowded beneath the broken arch of the Band Shell, mumbling and bobbing their heads.

"How did they get there?" Estra wondered.

"They didn't fly," he said. That much was sure.

Arden regarded her. "What now?"

"We're headed south."

"For what purpose?" he muttered. "To find a new sky to hide in?"

Estra sighed. Her eyes were sad.

"He's not going to give up," Arden said. "Is he?"

"No. He won't give up."

"Are we just stealing time for two souls that can no longer fuse? Pretending that our love is intact?"

His words distressed her. She turned into the breeze and let it blow her expression away.

"We could abandon the ship," he said. "Float away. Together or apart."

She stared at him.

"Are there people who do that?" he wondered. "Roam the sky on their own, like homeless spirits?"

Estra shook her head. "Without a sheltering cloud, the elements—sun, wind, rain—would dissolve you."

Silence. Then Arden met her gaze.

"We could return to earth," he said.

Despite all they'd been through, she looked stunned.

"You've been thinking about that?" Estra said.

"Would it matter?"

She turned toward the sun with a struggling smile, making herself translucent. "I could come with you."

He shrugged. "I wouldn't have any more power down there than I have up here."

At the end of the day, they stood together at the gashed and blunted Prow. Terra firma was in sight—a rugged mountain range, lined with dark buttresses. In the west, the sun was smothering, turning orange amid twists of smoke. The breeze played with Estra's locks, as if it meant to join them to the cirrus coiling over her shoulder.

"I hated my life as a toiler," Arden said. "But I don't belong here."

"In the sky? Is that what you mean? Or with me?"

He looked at Estra. "Do I seem like a child to you?"

She shook her head.

"I feel like one," he said. "Naive. Powerless. But clear enough to see the truth." He searched the empty air before him. "I'm not Ingis. I won't keep asking for More, when fate has decided that Less is my lot."

She put her hand on his shoulder.

"What is that?" Arden leaned forward. "Do you see it? There, right there."

Estra followed his finger.

"A bird," he laughed. "A tiny bird is crossing the gulf. It's lost or confused. The gulf is bottomless, a sea of mist. Is it— Yes, it's headed toward us."

Arden's bright tone was mixed with sorrow.

"Its path is straight. Its wings aren't broad enough to soar. It's just thrashing the air with everything it has. So much spirit and determination— Closer, closer—"

"Look at this," Arden said. "The little thing's halted in front of us. It's hovering above the gunnels, looking right at us. Those wings, purple and gold, sparkling like they were set with jewels. Its fiery eye, the green curl on its crown—

"A bird like this has never been seen. It must be the only one of its kind."

Estra stared at the vacant air, somber, silent.

"Now it's above us," he said. "It folds its wings and dives. It's disappearing beneath the hull. Odd creature. Curious soul. Goodbye.

"He's gone, Arden said. "There's only the gulf now, the mountains and the endless sky."

Estra's eyes were brimming.

"What was his purpose?" Arden said sadly. "Maybe he came to hear my admission of defeat. To offer himself as a gift to you. A gift you'll remember."

The rim of the Vat was worn and crusted. The fog within was whirling, its spiraling surface furrowed gray and black.

Not even the Vat could help them now. They had come to wash the poison of Ingis away before saying farewell. Estra would help him find a Tunnel to return to earth. She would remain on the ship for a little while. Purging her trespass, she hoped, would let her make a fresh start. She meant to put Ingis behind her. "My weakness for him," she said, "only the Vat can erase."

She approached the Vat's rim, with Arden beside her.

"Fond moments, the tender ones, memories of sympathy and connection—" She swept her hand across her face. "I'll think of the times I fed his pride and his lust, the injuries I did to myself, for him."

She took a breath. "A deep scrub. Count to six. Make it seven. Slowly."

Estra curled her trunk over the rim. Her head touched the surface, and then the windings caught her shoulder and dragged her in.

Arden began to count. "One, two—"

She sank and resurfaced.

"Three, four—"

Estra was on her back now. He could see the dark solvent soaking into her.

"Five, six—" That's long enough, he thought.

He thrust his arms in and caught hold of her leg. Then he pulled her closer, circling her waist, stretching it as he lifted her out. Arden backed away from the Vat, dragging Estra with him. He knelt and let her shoulders down onto the quilted surface.

She lay there, twisted on her hip, arms spread, jaw slack, with a stare as lifeless as a storm-beaten scarecrow.

Too long, he worried. What have I done?

He raised her, holding her close, his lips to her ear. "Estra—"

Her head shifted.

"Can you hear me?"

His words fogged against her cheek. Her chest heaved, and the fog entered her nostrils like two white worms.

Estra shuddered. Arden raised her shoulders, and as he did, breath whistled between her lips and her eyes opened.

She regarded her body with confusion. Her puzzlement mounted when she lifted her head and saw him.

"Estra?"

Her eyes clouded with suspicion. She put her hand to his chest to ward him off.

"You know me," Arden said. Had her thoughts wandered? Had her memories of him been purged along with those of Ingis? Or instead of them?

Then relief showed on her face.

Her finger touched his chin. The cranes sounded, calling from the Pond. Over the port gunnels, the blue was curled with clouds, like a waste of shattered eggshells. "Is anything wrong?" she asked.

"No," he said, muffling his doubts. "Everything's fine."

How much had she lost? Which memories, which feelings—

"You were in the Vat," Arden said.

"The Vat." She nodded, as if remembering what the Vat was. "I don't know why," she shivered, "but I felt so alone." She sighed and nestled against him.

Did she remember her betrayal, and their decision to part? He touched the motes of her brow. She was as beautiful as the night they met. For him, Estra would always be the ideal. He would never meet another woman like her.

"Do you remember Ingis?" he asked.

Her gaze deepened. "Yes, I remember the man. He was in my thoughts for a long time. A cursed creature. I couldn't help him. Ruthless. Unredeemable."

She sensed his surprise. "Was he someone you cared about?" Estra asked.

Arden heard the Vat's foam bubbling in his ear. His head went under, and the solvent entered his temple. He was replaying the scenes he'd imagined—Estra in the Cranium, on the bed with Ingis, their motes fully mingled. He would see those searing images one last time, and then never again. Her soul, her spirit, her perfect embrace, the passion he imagined belonged to him—

Then his mind went blank.

When he returned to consciousness, he was on his back and he was quaking. Estra had hold of his legs. He could feel the Vat's cathartic expelling—not just from his head, but from every part of his body.

Finally the seizure ended and his frame went limp. His breathing slowed, and he felt a deep calm. His mind was like his cell in the ziggurat—dim and empty; a faint sound reached him—the window had opened and a breeze passed through.

"Arden."

He turned his head, parting his lids. The space before him was crowded with circlets, twirling spirals tight as fern heads, tiny things all uncoiling at once. Then the fern heads faded, and a woman's face rose over him, large as a sun.

"Are you back?" she said.

"Mariod," he whispered.

The woman blinked. Her hair shone gold. No, not Mariod. Whoever she was, she seemed glad to see him. Shreds of familiarity emerged from her eyes, and shreds from his mind rose to meet them. The ragged surfaces met, fitting together.

"Are you the woman I loved?"

She laughed. "Love has no past. Love is the future."

Estra, he thought. He sat up slowly.

Thunder sounded at a distance, like the tolling of a gong. Estra turned. At the brink of the sky, a black storm cloud rumbled. As they watched, a glowing taproot emerged, with tendrils that twitched like fingers.

A memory surfaced, and with it, a shrinking hatred of the electric webs, the sucking winds and the storm's silver hand. And the man who controlled it all. What was his name?

"Ingis," she said, reading the uncertainty in his eyes.

"He's looking for us." Arden pictured the Eyehole and the man standing inside it.

"I was close to him once," Estra said. "I thought I loved him."

Arden nodded.

"I helped him build his cloud," she said.

"You lived on it with him."

She drew a breath. "You're not leaving me, are you?"

"Leaving?"

"That's been troubling me." Her brow creased. "I don't know why."

A stuttering cry reached Arden's ears. A lone crane was circling above them, like an angel of faith. Its call for hope pierced his heart.

"I belong here with you," he said. "In the sky."

Warm hues had spilled from the sunset colorbox—paint for a kokanee, cloudberry jam or a soaring hawk's eye. The mists on the hollow's rim were tawny, and the Spindles were copper. Arden knelt at the base of a large one. Estra was seated before a cone nearby.

He reached into his chest, found the tip of his heart's desire, and drew it out. Estra did the same. He touched his line to the cone. It adhered, and the spindle began to turn. Estra's was turning too. The wishing lines emerged from their chests.

They had risen from the quilting beside the Vat and wandered the ship, reacquainting themselves with it. Memories returned to each, confused and in pieces. Together they sorted and joined them, bridging the gaps, reconstructing the pursuit by Ingis, Estra's misstep and Arden's bold rescue. Some events and feelings were beyond recall, and that unnerved them both;

but the Vat's mercy came at a price. Finally, when they were ready to face their future, they'd headed for the Spindles.

"Back away," Estra said.

Arden stepped back, feeling the wishing line creasing his heart.

"Farther," she said.

"I'll break it."

"Wishing lines don't break," she said.

He took another step back. The line was taut, dripping and creaking.

"What do you see?" she asked.

Arden peered into the green mists. "I want to change things."

"What things would you change?"

"I'd stop running from Ingis," Arden said. "I'd face him. Fight him."

"You're wishing for power," she said.

"Power enough to throw him down," Arden agreed. "And you?" He eyed her wish collector and the green puffs around the line it had pulled from her chest.

"To be free of him, for good," she said.

There was a fierceness in Estra's voice he hadn't heard before, and her eyes had a look that was unfamiliar.

"I wish for daring," she said. "To silence my dread, to bury my softer side. To let nothing stand between me and that goal."

As he watched, surprise lit Estra's face, as if an answer was dawning.

"Together our wishes point the way," she said.

"Toward what?"

"A larger cloud." Estra touched her line, and a high note trembled the air. "His power grew with Ingishead. That storm is as much my creation as his. Our Practices built it."

"Practices?"

"A simple answer," she said. "It didn't hit me till now." She looked past the Spindles, scanning the ship fore and aft. "We'll grow. We'll build a storm of our own, big enough to do battle with Ingis."

7

They were on the Glitter Deck, standing by the gunnels. Far below was a flesh-colored desert bounded by brown peaks. Shreds of fog trailed beside the hull.

"We called this Practice 'Cannibals,'" she said. "It may not make sense at first, but after a while, you'll get the idea. It starts with a drink." She regarded Arden. "You're ready?"

"I think so."

"I'm closing my eyes. You'll need to close yours."

"They're closed," he said.

"I'm lowering my hand over the side, scooping some fog from the cannibal breeze." Her voice was hushed and theatrical. "The sky is haunted by cannibal devils."

"Devils?"

"I'm bringing my hand to my lips and drinking," she said. "Now I'm getting a draft for you. Here it is."

Arden felt her hand by his lips.

"Swallow it down," she said. "Fill your belly."

He sipped.

"I hear crazy voices," she said, "far away. Now they're closer. Terrible voices, more and more of them—howling, chanting in my ear."

Arden laughed to himself. The Practice was some kind of game.

"You can look at me now," she said.

As he opened his eyes, he heard a groaning and gagging. Estra was hunched a few feet away, turning a circle, her face a twitching mask, mouth in a silent howl, making hooks of her fingers and reaching for him. He laughed again, this time out loud.

"Don't make me regret this," Estra said.

"Sorry."

"I'm the cannibal," she said. "You're my prey. You're going to run for your life."

Arden took a breath and nodded.

"Alright," she continued. "Close your eyes."

He did as she asked.

"Let your imagination loose," Estra said. "I'm not acting. I'm no sweet thing. There's nothing tender about me. I come from a deadly tribe. I'm a monster, a beast— Can you hear my people behind me, spurring me on?"

Arden imagined the chanting voices with drums pounding beneath.

"I'm not just hungry," Estra said. "I'm starving. If I don't eat you, I'll die."

The savage babel filled Arden's head, raving in an alien tongue.

"Your time has come," she said. "Open your eyes."

She was hunched and seething, her face a grisly mask. She wrenched and reeled, as if her bowels were twisting. Her hooked fingers drew out, like claws—

Estra hurled herself at him, their bodies clashed and her claws dug in. He could feel them shredding his body, tearing through layers of vapor. Her eyes drilled, her chest heaved, her mouth gaped and her tongue twisted.

Arden tore himself free, fleeing across the blazing deck. The mad hunter was right behind him, huffing, snarling, fueling his terror. The sun was blinding, white to closed lids, a dazzling mirage to open ones. Her claws raked his back. Greedy sounds rattled in her throat, furious, incoherent.

She sprang, grappling his sides. They rolled— Her jaws clamped his neck. She gripped his bicep and tugged his arm off. Her hand drove into his middle, raking and clawing his jellies. Estra was ravenous. She devoured his pieces in a frenzy, wolfing them, swallowing them down. His boneless limbs, his vaporous innards, his foggy heart—

When she was done, he was all inside her. She was full to groaning.

Vapor freed the spirit, but freedom like this was a terrible thing. Arden felt a fear unlike any he'd known. He was still fully conscious, but he was moving through Estra, making a goosenecked exploration of her deepest recesses. She was digesting him.

"Calm yourself," she whispered. "It's almost over."

What calm could there be? His motes weren't mingling with hers. She was taking them from him.

"Let yourself go," she groaned.

Arden felt her fall to her knees. She was crawling, shuddering, sick and faint. He was still alive. His motes were squirming inside her.

She grabbed her middle and retched, delivering him onto the deck in a pile.

Arden felt the sun and the breeze. He was a jumble of macerated motes.

Estra bent over him. "It's your turn."

Bits of his head were migrating toward each other. His brow lifted, scarves adhering.

"You don't need to put yourself back together," she said. "You can make a meal of me as you are."

A meal—of Estra?

"I'm your victim," she said.

He had his tongue and throat back. "I don't want that," he croaked.

Her eyes narrowed. "Victim!" she cried.

Arden fought his repulsion and pushed his reassembling head toward her. His jaws opened, and he mashed her leg. Estra flinched, repulsed and fearful.

He wrenched his jaws, pulling her down. His head slid over her middle, and his jaws closed again, this time on her breast. Her hands scrabbled, but she couldn't detach him.

He worked his jaws, as if he was nursing. Estra bucked and thrashed. His head swelled and his neck grew longer. He was swallowing Estra's moted flesh, and as his appetite grew, his own moted parts congealed and drew together, making him whole again—strong enough to stand.

He hooked his fingers, yielding to his craving. "I'm starved," he warned her.

Estra trembled before him, tempting, helpless.

Arden lunged and she jumped, stumbling across the blazing deck.

She was the prey now, panicked and weak.

He halted, letting her go. That's enough, he thought.

Estra turned and raged, "You rabbit, you daisy—"

Arden threw himself at her and tore her to pieces. As he bolted her down, a growl sounded below. The ship shook. The hull seemed to twist. The growling mounted, along with a grinding, as if the ship too was starved and keen to be fed.

Estra struggled inside him. He could feel her parts moving, softening, dissolving. He opened his jaws, and her voice emerged, swamped and pliant. "What have you done?" she cried.

Suddenly it seemed that lust and love had returned to his life. Arden felt, once again, the unity he craved. His soul brimmed with the fullness of mingling motes. Estra was his, unquestionably his. And the rapture he felt—it had come without giving anything up.

A shiver of fear. Had he hurt her?

"Don't worry about me," she answered. "Look at yourself."

His hands were swollen. His arms, his legs— Nourished by Estra's motes, his body was growing.

"I'm larger," he murmured, understanding. This was the triumph a storm enjoyed—the point of the Practice.

"Your time's almost up," Estra said. "The devourer's gut is the cradle of power. I will be born," she proclaimed. "I will play god, and I will feast."

His stomach churned. He grabbed his belly and emptied its contents onto the deck.

As the pieces of Estra drew together, he saw with dismay that his body was shrinking, collapsing back. He was small again. But the thrill of growing—that was something he wouldn't forget.

They played Cannibals until the light expired. Then they dragged themselves back to the Bridge, collapsed on the deck and fell asleep in each other's arms, dreaming of the meals they had made of each other.

The two of them stood amidship, by the port gunnels, admiring the view. White vanes of cloud louvred the sky, and light flashed through.

"Can you hear it?" Estra said.

In the quiet, a faint growl reached them.

"Every cloud has a primitive gut," Estra said. "For most, it remains dormant until they die."

The Chamber, Arden thought. The vibration trembled the motes of his feet.

"The ship's Gut is stirring now," she said. "It awoke during the Practice. It's somewhere below."

"I've seen it," he said. "I didn't know what it was."

He led her aft, and when they neared the mizzenmast, he found the sinkage covered over with scarves. Together they peeled them off. As the misshapen well appeared, the growling grew suddenly louder.

"The place isn't safe," he said.

"We'll be cautious. I want a look."

She stepped into the well and levitated down. Arden followed.

The air was humid, the walls of the well were beaded and sweaty. As the Chamber opened around them, Arden saw it had grown. The basket was twice his height and twenty feet wide. Its cords of mist were spinning, and the uneven weave was flexing at every angle.

"Don't touch it." He spoke above the rumble and growl.

"You can see how hungry it is," Estra said. "It's waiting for something to digest."

Arden watched the loose web tense and relax, bulging and pouching like a spider web distorted around a struggling victim. There was nothing inside it, but them.

"The cloud wants to be fed," she said.

Estra took a breath and faced him, as if she was ready to disclose something she'd known for a while. "Something happened here, while I was gone."

"What do you mean?"

"You were piloting without manning the Bridge."

"So?"

"The cloud isn't ours now, Arden. It's yours."

Her words troubled him. "You brought us here. The cloud belongs to both of us."

"The cloud is yours." She spoke softly, with resignation, as if she wished it was otherwise. "It's hungry, and we're going to feed it. You're going to eat other clouds. Small ones to start. Then larger ones."

"The Practice stirred me," he said. "But I woke up feeling bad about it."

"We don't have any choice. We need to get bigger. Much bigger, if you're going to stand up to Ingis."

"The story you told me— About the night you learned what it meant to be a predator—"

She frowned. "I don't remember that."

"I can't forget it. Estra— I'll hate myself."

She sighed. "That's the way it should be. Enjoying the slaughter would be monstrous."

"I'll turn into Ingis," he said.

"Never. Not you. Growing won't change you. I feel that in my heart."

He peered into her eyes.

"I don't know any other way of doing this," Estra said. "We'll be careful. I'll be strong. We won't let things get out of hand."

"No people," he said.

She shook her head. "We're not going to eat any people. Just clouds. We'll scout our prey carefully."

Her assurances calmed some of his fears. But he was still troubled.

"Don't worry," she said. "We're in this together. We love each other."

"We'll always be equals," he said. "You're the wiser. You're the one with the long view."

"Consumption leads to power, Arden. That's what the feeding's about. It isn't just better to be bigger. If a cloud eats enough other clouds, it becomes a storm. It's the friction, ice and wind and vapor tumbling together— That's how a charge is brewed.

"We'll raise a storm that we'll both be proud of. Fearless, strong. With enough juice to stand up to Ingis. But human still. Human and self-aware. A storm that waters the land without flooding it, that uses its power to make the world a better place."

She lowered her eyes. Arden embraced her.

"We'll drive Ingis off," he said, "and shrink our cloud back. Or find a smaller one, and let the wind carry it."

Arden put his hands on the rail of the Bridge and edged the ship from behind the lens-shaped cloud where they had stalled it the previous night. The cloud was dense and pol-ished, and there was no seeing around it. As they glided from its lee, Arden saw the drifting scud they had spied from the top of the mast.

The growl of the Chamber mounted. He could feel the vibration up through his knees. Arden steered the ghost ship toward the scud. It wasn't much larger than one of their billows—white and puffy, and full of air. From the mast, he and Estra had checked to see if anyone was aboard.

She stood beside him, scanning the horizon for Ingis. "Go ahead," she whispered. "Head straight for it."

"And then what?"

"It will be like holding a perch under the nose of a cat," Estra said.

Arden steeled himself, gripped the rail and focused his attention. The ship powered forward. "Do you see anyone?"

"No. There's no one."

The deck streamed, the tendrils of the Hanging Garden trailed back.

"Faster," she whispered.

The port bulwarks shed flying skeins. As they approached the scud, the Prow trembled. All at once the foredeck lifted and the bows dropped, gaping like the jaws of a fish.

"It's yours," Estra said.

With a fierce suck, the ghost ship engulfed the scud. All that remained were tats of mist.

Choking sounds rose from the bows. Arden felt the lit-tle cloud shudder as it awoke to misfortune. And then it was

166

struggling. The ship's foreparts shook, and a moan echoed up from the Prow. Arden felt the scud's fear.

The cranes rose from the Pond, alarmed, stuttering to each other.

The scud wrenched and heaved. Was it caught in the ship's throat?

Estra put her hand on Arden's. "It won't take long," she said, and she drew his hand from the rail.

The ship slowed. The Bridge juddered beneath his feet. He imagined the scud passing through the ship's chest, into the waiting Chamber. The growling mounted, and a rasping grew out of it. Crushing, grinding—

"It's being digested," Estra said.

This was Cannibals, in real life. The woven basket was compressing, shrinking and clenching, crushing the cloud, releasing its wind and water. The Bridge was suddenly warm to Arden's feet.

"Brace yourself," she warned.

Large bubbles of air rose through the deck, ruffling the billows and thrumming the rigging. The ship wallowed and tipped. Its topside boiled, mushrooms of fog lifting from every surface. The Hanging Gardens collapsed. The mizzenmast melted. The Lofts erupted, and the Vat caved in, its contents hissing and coiling into the air. Would the blooming destroy the craft? As Arden watched, the hull's girth swelled.

"We're growing."

"It's almost over," Estra said.

The ship quaked, then seemed to steady itself.

Arden raised his hands from the rail and took a step back. He drew a breath and put his palm to his brow. "That was brutal."

Estra looked shaken. "The fruit from an ancient vine," she muttered. "I'd forgotten."

"The scud suffered."

She stared at the Prow. "You did what you have to do. You're not a cruel man." She edged between him and the helm, facing him directly. "Our enemy is without scruples. Ingis has no peaceful corners, no fair judgments, no considered opinions. He wants. He needs. He never shrinks. He expands."

Arden looked into her eyes.

"No moral sense trammels Ingis," she said sadly. "He has no honor to defend, no labor for love, and no reason for any. He lives to hunt. To feed and to grow."

"That's a terrible life," Arden said. "Isn't it?"

She was looking past him, at the base of the mizzenmast and the opening of the misshapen well.

"The sky is a dangerous place," Estra said.

They'd been running down clouds night and day, and the ship was much larger. Its masts and sails were gone, as were the Pond, the Lofts and the Spindles. The Prow was blunt as a shark's head, and the hull was burly. On the deck amidship, boils had built an ashen hill, and a new Bridge was perched atop it. Arden and Estra slept there, and they slept in shifts. When they weren't hunting, one was watching for Ingis. The cranes came and went, roosting in a pocket near the ship's nose. The malformed ones had dragged themselves to a flume by the stern.

The ship's gullet was massive now. Prey slipped easily down it, large and small. Soft clouds were digested quickly in the Chamber's muscular basket; icy ones took grinding and wringing, but the yield was more substantial. With every new quarry, the craft expanded.

There had been other Practices—"Make Me an Idol," "Too Big to Please," "Peace No More," and "Nursing My Rage." In the last, Arden focused on wounds from his past and magnified them. Estra kept the lessons coming.

His comfort with More grew. The bigger the ship, the more confident he felt; and the more confident he felt, the more he fed. The hunt sharpened his senses. He was like the falcons he'd seen on earth. Stalking was pure calculation, but once he was closing on prey, fury took over.

The cranes, as always, had a mind of their own. Often they would fly ahead, crying and circling over the victim. Afterward, whether the hunt was successful or not, they would plane around the Bridge, hectoring him, wings sickling the air. It was as if they imagined they were his moral betters and had taken it upon themselves to call him down. Did they think he was cold and heartless, arrogant, cruel? Estra ignored them, and he tried to as well. But he had moments of doubt and self-reproach.

They were feeding on smaller clouds, about to engulf one, when Arden spotted a woman in the stern, trying to tame her luffing billows.

Her body glowed, and when she stood, the sun shone through her. Their eyes met. She raised her hand. A bashful wave, like an opening clam, then her smile turned to terror. The growl from below was suddenly deafening. Estra grabbed the rail and wrenched the ship to the side, but its jaws took the woman's bows and left her screaming, blanched and bobbing, clinging to the remaining half of her craft.

"What are you thinking?" Estra faced him. She was shocked.

"I wasn't paying—"

"You almost swallowed her."

The fear in her eyes frightened him. "The ship," he muttered.

"You don't want to do that."

"No," he agreed, "I don't."

"A body's vapor can be digested, but the soul has its own life."

He replayed her words, unsure what they meant. "Where do souls go?"

"If you eat them, they stay with you."

"There are souls inside Ingishead?"

Estra nodded. "The Cranium's haunted by them."

An inland lake was below, burnished, distorted by snaking tides. The swollen ship cast a shadow on it—a bloated image in an ominous mirror.

On the Bridge, Arden turned and asked Estra about lightning.

"Once the ship has a charge, how will I control it? How does Ingis fire his bolts?"

She put her finger to her temple. "It all happens here." She looked ahead. "Let's not get distracted."

They were approaching a tribe of clouds all moving together, like an immense school of fish—thousands of cumuli, evenly spaced. The clouds were big, some bigger than the ship.

"There's the prize," Estra said, pointing at the largest, a boiling mass at the school's edge.

Arden focused his attention. "Can we get our jaws around it?"

The cloud's billows were shingled, like feathers on a bird's breast. The ship raced toward it, fog devils whirling on either side. As the jaws opened, Arden saw—they couldn't swallow the cloud whole. They'd have to tear it to pieces.

The billows swelled before him, round and lush—frothing egg whites, mounds of spun sugar— He felt the damp on his face, and saw droplets collect on his arms. The ship clove through the cloud's middle, sucking cold vapor down its throat.

He wheeled the craft for a second pass, but before he'd completed the turn, the first load of vapor reached the Chamber, and the ship rumbled and shook. The bows curdled, folding toward the Bridge; over his shoulder, the same thing was happening aft. It felt like the ship was coming apart. Stutters and shrieking—the cranes took wing, headed toward the lake's far shore. Estra's head bowed, looking down.

Beneath the Bridge, the ship's topside had erupted. A giant boil was rising, bearing them up, sucking fog from both ends of the ship. As Arden watched, the nose and stern shrank.

"Hang on—" Estra fell to her knees, gripping the rail's stanchion.

Arden knelt beside her. The rumble was deeper now, and the boiling was black—he could see it beneath them, through the perforated deck—black with a green sheen, like a carrion bird on the forest floor, doubled over and feeding.

The black boil was growing taller and taller, carrying them into the air. All the energy of the prey being digested was pushing from beneath. Dark vapors swirled around the Bridge. Arden reached out his hand. The caustic fumes burnt his palm. The roar mounted below, along with the drumming of wind and the cavernous echoes.

"The Chamber," Estra cried. "It's expanding."

If the Chamber still existed, it was the only surviving part of the ship. The rest had been sucked into the towering boil. Air was whirling inside it and around its perimeter. The column was thronged with hisses and whispers, and it leaned as if to balance its growth.

Amid the churn, Arden saw sparks. A thorn of light, a jittering thread, a compass-burst— Then a luminous weaving appeared, knotted and snarled—the tendrilled filaments of a head bulb from some other world.

Estra's eyes met his.

"We've got juice," she said.

The grinding mounted. The Chamber was digesting the entire ship, converting all the vapor it had ever possessed or consumed—

Arden's body tingled, his motes were bristling. Electric needles pierced his face and chest— And then: it was as if the dark boil had cracked, and a blinding light was advancing through it. His flesh thrummed with current, spasms in every mote—

Then the charge retracted. And as the spasms faded, he felt the gift of change.

New senses, new thoughts— A new emotional balance— As if the surge of power had rewired him. Estra was staring at him, as if she could see it. As if the jolt from the green-black boils had fashioned some new, magnified man. A dark idea bloomed in Arden's mind. His attraction to her from the very beginning— Half of her magic, half her allure, was her acquaintance with power.

The promise in Estra's eyes dimmed. "Trouble," she said, looking through him.

Arden turned.

Thirty degrees off the port bow, Ingishead was starting across the lake. Its anvil was tilted toward them. Rivers of rain poured from its Jowls, and a herringbone of birds glided beside its cheek.

"Cranes," Estra murmured, rising to her feet. "They're still with him."

Arden heard the surprise in her voice. He stood. She's remembering how the birds were created, he thought.

"You've got to drive this thing," Estra said. "It's your beast."

He put his hands on the rail. The giant tower responded, pivoting.

With air currents whirling on either side, he piloted the remade cloud over the lake, away from their pursuer. Estra stood rigid beside him.

"Faster," she said.

He could hear the wind chugging in Ingishead's throat, and when he looked back, the Cranium was crackling and glowing. From the swollen head, rain fell in torrents, and the interlaced cords of its neck were trailing behind. Arden feared the megavolt juice, but— Ingishead was an inspiring sight. Majestic. Godly. The cloud Arden was driving had no head, and it was half its height.

"We have to go faster," Estra urged him.

They were moving at high speed, but not as high as Ingishead. The storm's thundering surged in his ears, enormous, threatening, eclipsing the rumble beneath him. The dark Eyehole was fixed and glaring. Sheet lightning flashed, silhouetting Ingis—he was standing there, watching him.

"We have electricity," Arden said.

"You don't know how to use it," Estra replied.

A claw reached out from the Cranium, hissing and silver-blue. It fell short of the tower. Another bolt fired, and another. Both flashed to the side, but the next one tore through the tower's middle. The Bridge blew back. The tower

174

groaned and folded like a leg bent at the knee. Arden and Estra were lifted, legs in the air, clinging to the rail. The cloud boiled, trying to unbend itself, but another bolt cut through its middle, sending sheets of rain and gouts of white streamers flying.

The tower roared, raising fresh billows, healing its gashes. It re-erected itself, lifting the Bridge, returning it to level. Upright again, Arden pushed their speed.

Through the claps and booms, stuttering sounded. Arden's cranes were wheeling above him, forming a wedge, flying straight toward Ingis, mobbing the Eyehole, clouding his view. Are they on my side, Arden thought, finally? Now that I'm electrified. Or were they protecting Estra?

He drove the tower with as much force as he could, trying to gain some distance while he had the chance. Below, the lake's far shore was approaching. Behind, Ingishead was growing a pointed chin. From where the clawed cheeks melted into its neck, a vortex descended, spinning down, touching the water.

A bolt fired at the tower and missed. The cranes mobbed the Eyehole again, but the gap between the two clouds was closing. "We have to do something," Arden said. Estra was fixed on the sky ahead.

A bolt struck below the Bridge. Another winged it, dashing out sheets. Electric judders shook Arden's frame, shaking, shaking, refusing to let go. Winds came fiercely now, sweeping the ripped pieces toward Ingishead's neck. Then the vortex lifted, dumping the water it had sucked from the lake, flooding the tower, trying to fell it. We won't survive this, Arden thought. The torrent streamed down the tower's sides, dissolving its vapor, making it sag. The storm winds were pulling off clumps, eating its base. The tower's current flickered, retreating within.

Arden could feel Ingishead's charge mounting. His heart buzzed and his fingertips snapped. A current arced from Estra's chin to her navel.

The Cranium loomed over them now, brow jutting, cheeks streaming, temples winged. A sucking wind tugged the Bridge toward Ingishead's neck.

"Leave us alone," Estra shrieked.

Silver light splashed her face, while the sooty motes blackened her body.

In the Eyehole, Ingis leaned out, glaring—jealous, triumphant, tormented, cruel— Arden recalled the moment of Mariod's death, when all he could hear was the electric ratchet, like an executioner grinding his teeth.

"I'm taking you back," Ingis boomed. "I was crazy to trust you. This time you won't leave. I'll make sure of that."

Then he turned to Arden. "You don't know Estra. She's fickle, heartless. She's filled your ears with lies. Just like she filled mine."

"You've lost your senses," Arden shouted.

Ingis leered. "Let's see how you do when you're in the Jowls."

Ingishead's giant beak opened, glinting, descending to pick Arden up.

The cranes from both clouds mobbed Ingis together, shrieking.

Estra eyed the depths, as if she was going to jump. The Cranium thundered and blazed like the sun, and a dozen bolts drove straight down, hissing and glowing, circling the Bridge like prison bars.

"Swallow him," Estra raged at Ingis, "and take me too."

She moved against Arden, her hip merging with his, her shoulder, her thigh. "Eat my soul," she dared Ingis. "I'll torment you for the rest of your life."

Then her chest and her head overlapped Arden's, and their motes were fully mingled.

The great beak froze in midair. The winds died.

Ingis stared at the lone body on the Bridge, stunned, speechless.

Fear and shame— Arden's face felt raw. *Go*, Estra said.

He grasped the sagging rail. The crowns beneath him were rolling, the tower's peak expanding, as if some last hope were shaping its boils. The half-eaten Bridge teetered and rose.

Faster, she cried. Arden focused on maximum speed.

Behind, Ingis followed, slowly at first. Then his shock dissolved, and his rage returned.

Estra emerged, sliding out of Arden's body. She swung half around, checking behind them. "Here he comes."

"A heat band," Arden said.

Estra fixed on the way ahead. Beyond the lake, the earth was level—a nuclear desert with craters and sand. The air was striated above it, buttery, hazy with heat.

177

"Head for it," Estra said.

Arden drove toward the band. "Are you sure?"

"Faster!"

He powered the tower directly at it.

"We may not clear it," he said.

As they approached, the sky around the band loosened and puddled. He raised his shoulder and bowed his head, shielding his face from the heat.

Where was the burning edge? Would it lop the Bridge off?

A sizzling reached his ears. He could hear Estra gasping— The heat singed the motes of his head and shoulders.

Estra screamed, then her scream turned into a sigh.

Arden looked back. The heat band was blazing behind them. They had passed just beneath. Behind it, he saw a distorted image of Ingishead, barreling forward at full speed.

"He has to stop."

"He's out of his mind," Estra said.

As they watched, the storm cloud drove into the band, and the sky exploded with rain and hail. Bolts, lunging swords— A gray deluge, and a rasping gale.

He's passed through it somehow, Arden thought. Then he saw: the shimmering giant had been cut in two.

"Is he dead?" he wondered.

Estra stared at the divided storm, speechless.

The heat band had severed its neck. The Cranium was floating free, above the band, while the flexing neck shifted below, as if trying to find it. Billows emerged from the sheared surfaces.

Arden could see: the two halves of Ingishead were creeping together. Reattaching.

That night Arden dreamt that the majesty of Ingishead was his. For days, weeks, even years he had been piloting the storm across the sky. It was dark, and he lay sleeping on the giant bed in the boudoir, with Estra beside him. Through the Eyehole, the stutter of cranes reached him. They were riding the currents that circled the Cranium, gliding as one.

He could feel Estra's warmth. Still asleep—still dreaming—he rolled over to embrace her. But it wasn't the softness and frailty of vapor he touched. His hands felt knobs and pits and ragged edges. And when he opened his eyes, what he saw in the moonglow wasn't Estra's shapely form. It was Mariod's blackened corpse. Her body lay stiff and lifeless in his arms; and her face, once so warm and welcoming, was charred and crumbling.

8

*A*rden woke to see Estra beaming.

He raised his shoulders. Her eyes brimmed with wonder and excitement. She stood a few feet away, on the remains of the Bridge. Behind her, and on both sides, was a vast expanse of sky.

"You've done it," she said, holding out her hand.

He grasped it and stood.

She moved to the edge of the half-eaten Bridge and stepped off, spreading her arms, sailing from the rounded crown of the cloud and gliding away from it. Arden followed.

A draft carried them laterally. Then Estra wheeled, banking into the wind, and did a front flip. She emerged from the flip, belly down, legs flexed, arms spread, descending slowly. He did the same.

The top of the tower appeared before them—its rounded crown covered by a thatch of misty scarves. Below that, the cloudy boils dropped steeply, cut by horizontal creases. A large eave jutted out. Like a man's brow. And then Arden saw, rising toward him, the knurl above a giant nose.

The column of cloud had a head now—swollen, gigantic—with a sculpted face.

Its eye orbits were vacant, but the lids were combers that ticked with the wind. He and Estra were descending to one side of the giant nose. Its beam was broad, and a billow jutted like a giant cowling where the nostril flared.

"Can you see?" Estra said.

He could see. The face was his.

The cowling swelled and relaxed. There was wind in the nostril. The brow furrowed and the cheeks were hollowed, as if the effigy was confused.

Arden stroked with his arms, giving himself some distance. When he turned again, the face was calmer. The bust was his, but it was inky, not pale. Like the storm Ingis rode, the severed head ended in a neck impossibly long. Veins and connectives hung below it, bundled around a twisting spine.

"Ardenhead," Estra said, floating beside him. "What do you think?"

He spread his arms. "It's magnificent."

Which was Arden? he thought. A strange question. He was still small, still a man. But the giant cloud had some of him in it. As he studied the face, its brow lit up, flashing and crackling within. And the power lit Ardenhead's features. Strength, he saw. Pride, confidence and command—

"From determination and practice," Estra said, "a storm has been born."

"There's an opening," he pointed.

His storm had a mouth, and the giant lips were parted. The lower protruded—enough to make a landing platform.

Arden sculled and slowed, letting his legs swing down. Estra did the same, and together they set down on the lip.

It was smooth and seamed, with wisps and curls at its edge. On either side, Ardenhead's cheeks were smoking.

"A balcony," Arden said.

"Your helm," she nodded. "Your place of command, like the Eyehole for Ingis."

Estra regarded him, flush with hope, but nervous too. Arden surveyed the sky like a teenager looking in a mirror, seeing the first signs of a beard.

He turned and embraced her, dizzy with gratitude, imagining a proud future. The Balcony was more than just steering and intention.

"Look," she said, turning to face the Mouth behind them.

The opening was toothed by fog pillars and fringed with mist. Inside was a large oval room.

Arden crossed the threshold.

The space was lavish. A large tongue-shaped bed abutted the rear wall. Quilting and pillows were heaped on either side.

"Our Salon," she said. "We'll sleep here. Look what's in the corner."

Half hidden by an accordion baffle was a Vat, with cranes

stilted around it. And beyond that was an archway, hung with veils.

As they stepped toward the arch, the cranes' bills rose from beneath their wings.

"Our words are still on them," she said.

He saw the fond remembrance in Estra's eyes.

Beyond the archway was Ardenhead's Vault.

It was half the Cranium's size, but opulent all the same. The domed ceiling was covered with traceries of rime, dints and stalactites arranged in waves and wheels, and starbursts like hands with icy fingers. Cupolas and grilled windows opened on every side.

Sun rayed through lancets and meshes, lighting the Vault's interior fog. Churned by drafts from below, hail and rain and diamond ice clashed. He could hear the crackling, see the embers and silver thorns; and he could sense the field, the incipient power, the electric webs strung through the fog.

What had happened? he wondered. Was it the dream of Mariod that had caused the cloud's head to grow? Was it their encounter with Ingis—something Ingis had said or done? The giant cloud they had eaten— Had the Chamber been digesting it all night? Or perhaps the head grew from some change in him. Whatever had caused it, he knew what the change meant.

"You look troubled," Estra said.

"There's a battle coming."

Her gaze grew somber. "It won't be long."

"He'll never give up."

"Never," she said. "In the end, he'll decide: if he can't have me, no one else will."

"We have electricity now."

She nodded and raised her hand, stopping an inch from his chest. "It's time."

He couldn't make sense of the look in her eyes. Was it dread or anticipation?

"You have to learn how to control it," Estra said.

She gazed around the Vault. Then she took his hand and led him to a cloister with a veiled sidelight. In the fog above, current winked and snapped.

"The charges in a storm cloud," Estra explained, "are jags passing from droplet to droplet, from mote to mote. The voltage mounts," she opened her palm, "with your emotion. If you're calm—just a few sparks. If you're violent—here comes a bolt. Good so far?"

Arden nodded.

"We'll start with a wire of current."

"Where do I get the wire?"

"Imagine it." She looked at the charges in the fog above. "It's your head."

"Should I close my eyes?"

"That's not required. Listen to the crackling. Imagine a glowing hair. You're pulling it through one mote after another, stringing beads on a thread. There are motes all around us, so a thread can go in any direction. Try it. Pull one toward you."

Arden frowned, focused on a hiss in a gallery nearby and imagined pulling a wire from it.

"You're stringing a path for the current to follow. You have one now?"

"I'm not sure."

"Concentrate," Estra said. "Send a wire to that pillow on the floor."

Arden pulled on the hissing charge, but nothing happened.

"Draw it out carefully," Estra said.

A glowing thread zagged through the fog, and its end sizzled on the pillow.

"Good," Estra said. "Send one through the transom," she pointed, "but this time with passion."

Arden focused on a spark, drawing the current through the atomized vapor—up and up, toward the transom. The wire fizzled to one side.

"Vapor is a conductor," Estra said. "The current is looking for a path. Just show the current where you want it to go."

Arden tried again and again. The charges were thin and the voltage was low. The wires sputtered out, or zagged before reaching their targets.

"I can't feel your emotion, Arden."

"I'm not sure what you're asking for."

"Emotion," she said. "I know it's there. Let it out."

"I'm doing the best I can."

He strung another current, and another, but the wires just snapped and fizzled. There was nothing resembling a bolt.

"The energy is here." Estra motioned at the charges adrift in the Vault. "But the emotion is not. Fury, pride, passion, rage— There's something stopping you, choking you off. Let go of the reins. Take the lid off. What are you afraid of?"

Finally she called a halt.

"Let's sit down," Estra said. She seemed anxious, doubtful.

She stepped over to a pair of fog cushions, and lowered herself onto one.

Arden sat on the other, facing her.

"Alright," Estra said. "You're going to try it on me."

"On you?"

She nodded. "I don't want you to focus your emotions blindly. Direct them here." She patted her sternum.

"You're going to use electricity to move my body." Estra gave him a wooden grin and turned her head to one side and the other, by way of example. "Imagine that I'm your puppet. To move my arm, you'll have to connect wires to it. Here," she put her finger on her wrist, "and here, and here—" She touched her elbow and shoulder. "Let's try that first.

"Pick a spot on my arm. When I raise my finger, I want a surge of emotion, and at the very same time, look at the spot and direct your wire to it. Are you following me?"

"A surge of emotion," he nodded.

"I'm going to help you." Estra raised her finger. "I dreamt we were in our hammock last night, mingling our motes."

A wire shot through vapor behind him and landed on Estra's shoulder, jerking her arm.

"The school of clouds we saw over the lake," she said. "I want to eat them all."

Another wire jabbed her knee, and Estra's foot kicked.

"Better. A little." She regarded him. "The woman on the cloud— Her wave was an invitation to you."

A wire struck Estra's hip, joggling her on the cushion.

"You're provoking me," he objected.

"Yes I am," she fired back. "This is a Practice, Arden. We called it 'The Puppet.' I played it with Ingis all the time." She took a breath. "You've never had the courage to free your feelings the way he does. The last time you and I made love, I was thinking of him."

A glowing wire shot through the fog, ripped past his ear and pierced Estra's shoulder. She shuddered, and a twist of smoke rose from the spot.

Arden's hands were shaking. "You weren't really."

"Really, I was," she said. "How much do you hate him?"

Arden sent a thicker wire, but it bent against her thigh and winked out.

"I've hardened myself." She clenched her jaw and folded her arms. "You'll have to increase your voltage. If it's rage you need, then nurse it. You know how to do that."

She lifted her chin. "I'm not going to wipe your behind like Mariod."

Arden flung a much thicker charge—almost a bolt—and it drove through her throat. An arc sizzled across her breasts, and her feet rose on their toes. When her shuddering stopped, she drew a breath.

"That wasn't so hard," Estra said.

"I'm not going to do this," he shook his head.

She laughed. "Yes you are." There was scorn in her eyes. "You're worthless to me. You're a man that *wants* and never *has*."

He sent a bolt at her jaw, knocking her head to the side.

"Power," she said. The word groaned in her throat. "When his current went through me, I couldn't feel anything else."

Another bolt, and another—piercing her middle, buckling her trunk.

"It speaks," she rasped, "to every mote in my body. It must be obeyed."

"Stop," Arden raged, standing.

"It was the juice," she said softly, "that made it so hard to leave him."

The look in her eyes stopped his breath.

"Arden," she said with a pitying look. "You don't have the stomach for this."

He was speechless.

"Ingis would make his puppet go crazy," she said. "He wouldn't hold back."

Arden stared at her for a long moment. Then he launched an attack. A wiry leader split her thigh, raising sparks and smoke; one divided her head, flashing and prying; then *crack*, a bolt plowed through her chest and her middle vanished. Ripping, woofing—her ghostly body twisted and clenched, hunching forward and back. He pedaled her legs and scrambled her face; he thrashed her arms and seesawed her hips; he made a wicket of her back and put her hair on end. When he stopped, she slumped.

"Estra—" He gathered her in his arms.

She felt airy and disconnected, light as a duffel of down.

Her lids parted, seeing him as if from a distance. "Is this it?" she whispered. "Am I a puppet for good? Will I ever have control of myself again?"

Like a vat, dark and turning, her eye brimmed with desire.

He kissed her lips. His face lapped over hers, and their foreheads moted together. They sank into a quilt of fog, thick and prismatic.

In her heedless passion, Arden felt the unfolding of some kind of secret. Their legs joined, and then their arms. The Vault's wind rocked them, and its fog slid over them. His chest merged with hers. "Wire us together," Estra said.

Hearing crackles in the Vault above, he reached for a glowing thread, drawing it close to them both. He was one with her now, motes perfectly mingled, sharing their borders. He shot the thread, and it hissed through their middle. With one throat, they cried out; and they were shuddering together.

Estra's motes glittered, and so did his; her eyes were on fire, and they melted his own. He mustered another wire. She waited with bated breath. The "missing" passion—the thrill of shared circuits, the rapture with Ingis that Estra had felt— wasn't missing anymore.

He drove wires through them, then followed with bolts. The currents thrummed every bead, connecting every mote in their electrified body. And the spasms and judders freed the emotions she craved—the buried truth, the scathing feelings no words could express. Could a man with power like this be a protector? The juice frightened him. And it frightened her too. This was the Estra that had bowed down to Ingis.

"Say what you said to him," he gasped.

"Please—"

"Do it."

She caught her breath. "You're my destroyer—"

"More."

"My ruin, my A-bomb—"

Was she pandering to his ego? Did he care?

"King, you're my king," she said. "King of heaven, beholden to none."

Arden was a storm now—his pleasure high-voltage, life-threatening; his displeasure, worse. He was ruthless, cold in his essence. And Estra couldn't resist him. She was like he had never seen her. Her motes crept beyond his—airy, delicate, expanding at every angle. Her cheeks inflated. The sides of her face lifted over her brow. Sheaves slid from her middle, hands expanding like fans— She was coming apart.

Arden summoned a bolt—a giant one. It came crashing through them, electrifying every atom at once. He shuddered and glittered, coiling in smoke. Estra, dispersed and unstable, took the stroke like The Puppet's last act. It shattered her. She was nothing but a retreating cosmos of blasted motes.

After what seemed a long while, a figure recongealed in the fog beside him. Its chest rose and fell, drawing breath. A fresh scar, a white hook, was branded on its belly.

With a deafening *rip*, a bolt from Ardenhead drove through the failing storm's temple. Its brow burst, its crown sluffed and screws of smoke unwound from the remains of its head. Arden followed the stroke with a relay of electric feelers. He stood on the Balcony, driving silver threads through his prey, down the reeling storm's neck to ground.

When the battle began, the storm had been Ardenhead's size, but it was swooning now. Ragged shreds hung from its throat, slapping against sheets of rain as its currents discharged. The blind cloud kept firing, sending spokes in every direction, its crackling core like a terrified eye.

Arden conjured another bolt—from a floating charge, through a myriad motes in the Vault, and out through a half-dome window—stringing beads on the jags. When it struck, the base of the prey's head exploded, and the stump of its neck grew luminous fur. Abruptly, the cloud's thunder died. Its billows drifted, silent and shining, while orbs of blue fire bounced on the crowns, and electric plumes sprouted from fissures. The lingering volts were stranded now. The storm had been a giant, but it was finished. There was no need to further divide it.

Arden steered closer—close enough for the winds from Ardenhead's collar to sweep the drifting remains under its head. The Vault was much larger than it had been that morning or the day before; the neck was taller and thicker; and what had once been the ship's Chamber was a giant digestion cave in the storm's throat. As Ardenhead fed, the Throat boomed and the Vault quaked, boiling with vapor and cracking with juice.

Estra watched from the Salon. When Ardenhead began to lurch, she hurried onto the Balcony.

"That's too much," she said. "You know that."

"We're fine," he replied, hanging on to the rail.

The thunderhead's cheeks hollowed. A sound like wheezing came from the Throat.

"We can't breathe," Estra grabbed his arm.

"It's just wind and water," he dismissed her concern.

Suddenly the Throat seized, and the wheezing stopped.

Arden turned to face her. Was the spongy mass more than the basket could manage? Was the prey already crushed? An awful groan rose from below. Arden imagined the bolus swelling, bursting the cords of the basket, creeping through the constricted Throat like a rat through an adder.

Then booming resumed, along with a fierce quaking, as if the storm meant to consume the bolus, whatever the cost. He saw the fear in Estra's eyes.

"We're going to explode," she said.

All at once, the threat of extinction was real. He gripped the rail, backing abruptly. The billowing behemoth swayed and lurched. The storm's winds huffed now, expelling not sucking.

"Cough it out," he muttered.

Arden backed farther, and the huffing mounted. Estra gripped the rail.

The winds churned around them. The lurching turned convulsive.

The Balcony jutted. Above, Estra could see Ardenhead's

cheeks and brow distending. Lurching, heaving— And then—

A great steaming mass of ashen billows erupted below. Through a tear—a cockle like the ones below Ingishead's Jowls—the prey's ugly bolus, half digested, returned to the air.

As the Balcony settled, Estra shivered and sank against Arden. He embraced her, watching the charges in the regurgitated mass wink out.

"That storm was loaded," he said with regret, looking up at the rangy eave of Ardenhead's crown. "We would've gained another two thousand feet." Then a moment of acceptance. "You were right. I'm pushing too hard. Don't let me be reckless."

"It was going to be different," Estra said softly.

"We don't have a choice. You said it yourself. He isn't going to give up."

She nodded.

"Ingis isn't content," Arden said. "He isn't holding steady or shrinking right now. He's larger than the last time we saw him, and his head has more juice."

It would be small to argue, she thought. Ingis was on his mind every minute of the day, and he went to sleep fearing the next encounter. Arden had to build his strength. Their future would be decided in combat, and soon.

His striking accuracy had improved dramatically. They had hunted small storms at first, raising their sights as Ardenhead grew. With the Balcony as helm, they prowled the skies, Arden piloting while she scouted prey. "We're nearly as tall as he is," Arden would say. "Almost," she replied.

194

Estra put her hand on his chest and sobbed. Not a welling of tears, not even a drop. Just one dry gasp. "It isn't just Ingis," she said. "It's us."

They mingled their motes morning and night, with a fervor verging on desperation.

"The frenzy," she said, "the violence—"

"No man in the world would think you were acting."

"You know I'm not."

"It's as good as it was with him. Isn't it?"

Shame darkened her eyes. "Is that all that matters?"

He touched her cheek.

"I'm not Ingis," he said. "I'll never be Ingis. Once we're rid of him, we'll forget all of this and go back to our ship. The heart needs more than a jolt of electricity."

His words reached her. Her distress lightened. "I loved the Pond and the hammock," she said. "Our innocent ways."

Over his shoulder, a blood-orange miasma veiled the sun. The Balcony was their eyrie now. Even as the motes of their hips overlapped, she could feel his trunk twisting, scanning the world below. He was like a lord surveying his kingdom.

Arden's nerve had grown with his storm. It wasn't just overconfidence, and dangers like the one they'd just weathered. There were moments of arrogance, moments of scorn; a seething beneath the surface. Without saying anything, he had plotted a course to a rainy coastline. Crooked ridges rose in ranks, pointed with peaks, clothed with tall conifers. The latitude and climate looked familiar.

195

Estra drew a breath and spoke. "Why are we here?"

"Nostalgia, I guess." He regarded her.

He was trying to read her thoughts.

"All those years of my life," he said, "I lived like a beetle on the forest floor. Whenever boots sounded, I scuttled for cover. I'm captain now. Master of my fate."

"We're near the ziggurat?"

Arden turned back to the view. "It's on the other side of that ridge."

The settlement reacted as soon as Ardenhead rolled into view.

Arden followed their alarm from the Balcony. He seemed to enjoy it.

From what Estra could tell, any positive memories he might have had of the place were forgotten. And it wasn't hard to understand why. The hurried preparations were for an offering to occur at twilight.

Between two lines of electric torches, the cortege of priests and overlords filed onto the Apex summit and took their positions beneath the Colonnade. As a priest removed the young woman's clothing, Estra spotted her; and the boy, who was being disrobed a few feet away. Ardenhead was hovering close, but the litany barely reached them through the batting winds.

"In my dreams," Arden said, "the ziggurat's gigantic. Like a city of lights on the side of a mountain." His hand swept the view. "A million windows, and in every one, a toiler's face peers out." He looked down. "The real thing is as small as the day I left."

Estra watched him, wondering. What did he mean to do?

The naked woman and the young boy were led to their places. Estra saw the priest with the long black cable approach. She was raising the cable when Arden fired the bolt.

The crankled sword drove into Apex, and the Colonnade exploded.

Estra turned, dumbstruck, gazing at Arden. When she looked down again, the winds were clearing the smoke from the blackened hole. On the bottom level, people were pouring out of the ziggurat like ants from a threatened colony.

"Helpless," she muttered.

He tensed his lips without speaking.

"The woman and the boy," Estra said.

Arden was silent.

"Ingis was here." She stared at the smoking crater. "But he didn't do that."

Arden followed her gaze, drawing against her, oddly meek. "That should bother me," he said, "shouldn't it."

He sounded like a forlorn child. Estra felt like her heart would break.

"It should," she said.

An eel of fog was gliding over the Balcony. It skirted a puddle fed by a drizzle from Ardenhead's nose, paused by her foot, then made a slow circle around their legs while the two of them watched.

9

hree days had passed since the destruction of Apex.
Arden had driven the thunderhead west and made the
coast their hunting ground. Every day was a rampage,
spotting storms, running them down, striking and feeding.
Estra was committed to the mission. What was distressing, even
horrifying, in the menacing darkness, somehow made sense in
the light of day. As Ardenhead grew, her prospect narrowed.
And so did his. Size answered every question. Fury drove out
doubt. No qualms, no reservations—that was Arden's goal. To
be as ruthless as Ingis.

The storm had gained six thousand feet since they'd arrived, and Arden wanted six thousand more. Did he dread the
appearance of Ingis? Increasingly, he ached and itched for it.
"He's going to find us soon," he had said that morning, after a
bout of electrified love. Estra was no longer fighting her craving
for current. The frequent connections strengthened their bond.

It was the end of the day, and the sun was low. Ardenhead's face was scarlet, and the Balcony glittered with embers, as if a brazier had spilled across it. They were looming over a bantam storm, playing cat and mouse.

The little storm's billows were flaccid and pale. Its crooked wires poked out, tentative, missing more often than not. Arden bided his time, brewing his juice. Finally it was time to put the inept creature out of its misery.

Arden sent a bolt down, every atom buzzing along its path. It clove the sky with a deafening clap, dividing the fluff, lopping the storm's lily head from its neck.

Estra stood on the Balcony beside him, watching.

"The sun gives light and so do I," Arden laughed. "But not so merry."

Thunder sounded like a gong in the Vault behind them, and two glowing claws shot from opposite sides of Ardenhead's brow, converging on the drifting halves of the victim, tearing them to pieces. Torrents of wind and rain blew from Ardenhead's neck, battering and drenching the storm's remains.

"This one's ready to eat," Arden said.

His fists gripped the rail, guiding Ardenhead closer, winds whirling and catching the sundered pieces. He glanced at Estra. She was silent, but her eyes danced. Then Arden looked back at the meal, and his motes froze.

His hands jerked from the rail. His lips parted, then he raised his finger, pointing.

Amid the storm's soaked rags, a white boil floated. A human figure was kneeling on it.

"Is it a man or a woman?"

"I can't tell," Estra said.

Arden stared at the castaway. "It's a man. He doesn't know what he's doing."

"He's alone," Estra said. "If he wasn't before."

The man spotted them. He was lifting himself, waving his arm to hail them.

"Levitate," Arden murmured. But the man was unhinged by fear.

Arden's cheek twitched. His lips trembled. He returned his hands to the rail, and began to back Ardenhead away.

"You've destroyed his cloud," Estra said.

Arden turned to her. What good was the drifting vapor to a helpless man? Were they just going to let the wind bear it away?

Estra's eyes darkened. Her jaw went slack. Arden waited for words, feeling lost. Would he always be a toiler? he wondered. What was he doing? The power of love. The love of power. It was clear to him suddenly—how his path twisted and where it led.

He put his hands back on the rail, fixed on the tatters and powered Ardenhead forward. The fierce winds sucked the storm's pieces up, and the terrified man came with them.

Arden felt Estra's hand grip his arm. There was fear in her eyes, fear and guilt. And acceptance. "It wouldn't matter to Ingis," she said.

A rumbling started deep in the Throat. Ardenhead was making ready to digest what it had swallowed. Arden let go of the rail. He held his hands up, staring at them. Then he turned and raised his head, seeing his own giant features above him.

A strange sound reached him, high-pitched, warbling. The man's crying out, he thought. Trying to be heard over the rumbling. Was the sound outside his ear? Was the man's voice inside his head? *Save me, save me—* A trick of the mind, Arden thought. Or the haunting was starting.

"What is it?" Estra asked.

"I can hear him. The man's soul— Inside my head."

"That's not possible." She turned him to face her. "He isn't digested yet. His soul hasn't been released."

Save me, save me— He could hear the voice clearly.

"I'm going down there."

Arden wheeled, strode through the Mouth and crossed the Salon. Estra hurried after him. They passed the Vat and entered the Vault.

It was a startling sight at the end of the day, when the setting sun painted the walls. The arcades were peach, the cupolas ruby, and the open windows were blue. They could hear the roar and grinding below. Shreds of cloud were being crushed, and leaden billows were rising through the Vault's fretted floor, weighted by rain, clashing with hail,

studded with crackling thorns. The billows roiled toward the bowed ceiling.

Arden scrambled across a trapeze of fog, and on the Vault's far side, he followed a misty aisle around the jaw's curve. Estra raced to keep up. Did he think he could save the man? Did he imagine he could stop the Throat before it digested him?

Between the Throat's rumbles, Estra could hear the stutter of cranes. She watched the birds flash past the lancets, circling the Vault, sorrowful, grieving. If Arden was listening, she thought, he would think they were crying about the doomed man. He wouldn't understand they were mourning his strength, lamenting the loss of a weaker self.

Beneath a sooty cloister, the misshapen well descended, hung with dripping skeins. Arden stepped into it, arms at his sides, and levitated down. Estra followed.

The noise from the Throat was deafening. Winds spun in the well's narrow space. She avoided touching the walls, using her hands to filter the needles of ice from her breath.

At the well's bottom, the Throat opened before them, barely pierced by rays of red light. Arden set down, and she landed beside him. Over his shoulder, Estra saw the enormous basket contracting around its victim, grinding and crushing it. What had once been cords, thin as straw, were writhing columns, flexing tornados woven together, every one of them spinning. High above, where the basket tapered like an onion, the digested vapors rose toward the Vault's grated floor.

The niche where they stood was puddled and reeking. Arden sloshed forward, dodging the gusts, waving his arm to clear the haze.

"We're too late," Estra said. She followed, wheezing, gagging.

Arden stopped, gazing at the nightmare web as it pursed and clenched, cocking his head as if he was listening, trying to locate the voice he heard. A whine, a warbling whine— And then, all at once, it turned into a scream and Estra could hear it. The man was at the center of the tumbling bolus, limbs flailing, eyes wide as the basket collapsed. The compressing fog, greasy and iridescent, smothered his cry.

Estra had seen this evil before, but she had never been its author. Only Arden knew what it meant to be Ingis.

"Murder," Arden thought. But it was something far worse. He had eaten a man. Part of the man was becoming him, and part of the man wasn't. The man's energy was his now, but his soul was not. They were both going through the Throat.

Arden swung around, fixing on Estra. "His cry— Can you hear?"

"I can," she answered. "But not like you."

He faced the giant basket and spread his arms. "Ardenhead consumes and inflates its mass," he raged. "What does it crave? Search the sky. Everything feeds Ardenhead, including you and I. Is the woman I love listening? Is she sad? Is she pleased? Is there anything she'd like to say?" He turned back to her.

Estra was speechless.

As the basket loosened, the crushed bolus rose toward the Vault. It roared, and the warbling cry rose with it.

"Ardenhead is death and blindness," he said. "It's the void yawning wide—"

The sound of lunacy, he thought. A madman was playing hell on an organ—its bass pipes rumbled, and its trumpets screamed.

"It's time," Arden cried to the man's soul. "Give yourself

to Ardenhead. Scream if you like—scream, scream! You're headed for my Vault, and you'll never come out."

Estra sobbed and embraced him.

"What have I done?" Arden said.

"Maybe we serve a greater good," she mumbled, pleading.

Her words didn't make sense to him.

"We want to make an end of Ingis," she said, "but we aren't alone. What we're doing, we're doing for us. But— We may be the only chance the sky has to rid itself of him. Think of all those who will fall prey to Ingis, if we don't succeed."

Arden wondered if she was serious.

"Is that a foolish idea?" She wiped her eyes. "They're giving their lives for an important cause. A noble one."

"You don't believe that."

Estra was tight-lipped. She closed her eyes.

"What's happened to us?" he said.

"It's my fault." Her brow creased. "When we were over the lake— The things Ingis said— That I'm fickle. Heartless."

Arden remembered.

"You don't believe that," she said.

"He was trying to poison my mind."

"It was poison. Just poison." She peered at him. "You still love me?"

"I don't care what Ingis says or thinks."

A deep rumble sounded, from outside now, like an engine of torture rolling closer.

Arden sloshed through puddles to a porthole and looked out. On the western horizon, the sun was a fan with beams of gold, and the sky stretched across it like lavender fabric. Ingishead was centered in the fan, crown perfectly rounded —a vision of doom from the Age of Science. A cape of fog circled the base of its neck, like a crust of salt covering a lake. Ingis was starting across it, headed toward them.

They were about to levitate back up the well, when Estra pointed to a dim corner. There, huddled together, were the malformed cranes. They thought the birds had perished. Perhaps they had dragged themselves to the ship's Gut before it transformed.

As they crossed the Salon, a flash filled the Mouth.

Arden felt the charge as he had that night in the Bower. His face prickled, sparks spit from his fingers. A silver web crossed his chest.

He looked at Estra. She was sparking too.

Arden motioned her to stop and continued toward the Mouth, stepping out onto the Balcony alone.

A thick veil of mist obscured the view.

All at once, the electric presence was fierce.

Ingis is here, he thought. Arden could feel him in every mote. The monster, the magician was close. And moving closer.

A clap of thunder—the sky turned white. Then a bright weaving rose from the mist before him, flickering. And the giant Cranium rose with it.

Ingishead roared. The sound shook Arden's chest.

He saw the great storm in profile—its luminous crown, its wind-curled quiffs, its gleaming beak and its clawed cheeks. Ardenhead had grown. But the storm of Ingis was larger. Much larger.

The impossible mass of the Cranium staggered him. Beyond regal, beyond majestic. Ingis dreamt of a sky, Arden thought, with only one cloud—an empire spanning the heavens. Even the sun seemed impressed. It shimmered and fawned, dipping low, backlighting the storm with a slavish display.

Rivers of rain flowed down Ingishead's neck, braiding with the cords that trailed, like arteries and connectives, from the base of its severed head. Between thunders, Arden heard stuttering cries. The cranes of Ingis were wheeling, soaring and diving through the ashen billows, crying to him and each other.

Slowly Ingishead turned.

The Eyehole came into view.

Ingis was standing there, with the lightning flashing behind him.

The man was ghostly—translucent, like himself. He looked calm, unlike their last meeting. And his face was handsome, not monstrous—with a cleft chin, a straight nose and kindly eyes. His relaxed stance and his youth surprised Arden. Ingis was not much older than himself. He could have passed for a toiler on the sluice gang.

Ingis drew a breath, buckled his lip and took a step forward. His carriage and expression had an air of the inevitable, as if he'd been living with his struggle—for size, for Estra—so long, it was second nature to him.

He met Arden's gaze and smirked.

"Power and fear," Ingis said. "An unfortunate marriage. Power loves fear, and fear loves power; and the unfortunates are us."

A dazzling flash burst from Ingishead's crown. The sky crackled and the bright weaving reappeared—a ragged compass, with thick roots and shivering threads. Rain fell between them.

Far below, Arden saw a large bay. The forested coast was in the distance.

Estra stepped onto the Balcony. She paused, gazing up, taking in Ingishead. "You're a giant now," she muttered.

Her eyes found Ingis.

They stared at each other in silence. Then Estra moved along the Balcony.

The rain came heavily now. Below, the bay heaved, shattered by spume. Above, the sky was shattered by wires, loosed from Ingishead's crown. Between those unpuzzling worlds, Arden stood, naked and ready. Estra drew close, standing beside him.

Ingis appealed to her directly.

"With all our disharmony," he said, "the dream persists. The dream we shared—of a higher love and a higher mind—exalted, wiser, more powerful."

Arden was hearing it finally—the romance of Ingis.

"Have we lost ourselves?" Ingis asked her. "No. We're still here—"

Estra looked as if a nesting snake was making its home around her. Ingishead's juice crackled between every word.

"—still feeling that matchless transport, that precious euphoria." Behind him, the Eyehole flickered with fresh ideas.

Estra turned away.

"Answer him," Arden said.

She extended her hand and touched his cheek.

Arden drew her close and kissed her. They turned and faced Ingis together.

A cold wind reached out, clubbed him to the side and picked Estra up, grabbing and shaking her. Arden circled her leg, alloying their motes. Ingis cocked his head, and the fierce wind redoubled. A blast from another quarter joined in. Arden's hold was unyielding. He thought they would both be carried away. Shrill, harsh, terrible yearning— Was it her voice he heard? Was it Estra struggling? No. It was Ingis, the mad winds of Ingis—

Arden felt the hostile charge mounting—in his feet, his arms, his legs— Estra was outlined with sparks.

"Let her go," Arden threatened.

Bolts struck on either side of them—a blinding fork.

Arden's cranes exited the Vault, piercing its boils, crying, distressed. They dove for Ingis, filling the space with their fearless stutter, jabbing at him with unerring stilettos.

The wind lost its grip. Arden caught Estra in his arms. Her feet touched the Balcony, and he waved her down. As she sank to her knees, a bolt from Ingis shot out.

The light was brighter than any noon on earth, with a

209

rip no ear in heaven could endure. The stroke scattered the cranes and drove through the Mouth, birds tumbling around him as Arden convulsed. It was as if he had never seen or felt electricity before.

As the bolt retracted, there was shouting in Arden's ears. A flood of emotion, frighteningly close—

"Drowned lungs, silver trees—"

Was Ingis raving?

"Burnt dwarves, cannibal screams—"

Arden shuddered. He could hear the spit on great lips, the click of a tongue—

Above, the Cranium crackled, brewing another charge, flashes lighting the boils from inside. Estra's huddled body crawled with white squiggles. Behind him, Ardenhead heeled and plunged. Its upper lip had been snagged and torn away by the bolt Ingis had fired. Nothing remained but a broom of white streamers. Arden gripped the rail, focusing on a scatter of charges adrift in his Vault, drawing them through a myriad motes—

A fierce *crunch*. Light flashed across Ardenhead's face. A terrible rumbling behind the creased brow—

Swords lunged from Ardenhead's eyes, from its temples, its cheeks— They were aimed at the figure shifting in the Eyehole, but they landed above, below, to one side and the other, driving electric stakes through Ingishead's face.

Ingis returned his blows—wires, wires, and a thick bolt with trailing root threads above and below. The bolt struck the Balcony's corner, and Arden felt the jitter travel his spine. An unbearable buzzing bloomed in his head. "I know, I know," he rasped. And he thought he really did know. He was feeling his rage now, a heedless fury. To survive meant nothing, life had no purpose other than this: to see Ingis burn and blacken, to destroy and consume him— Rain in slashing sheets joined Ardenhead's shots, but still Ingis stood, untouched, firing back.

Someone shouted in Arden's ear. Estra was close, jittering in the strobe. He pushed her away, and the contact made her dance like a puppet. His body was glowing now, every nerve on end. The air flashed, the sky tipped. Bright wires glittered and shook, linking the two raging storms and their livid faces. Then Ingis connected.

A crooked leader touched Arden's shoulder, and the juice took hold of him, heaving him up and casting him down, freezing and burning, filling his chest and wrenching his jaws.

As he struggled to rise, an agonized roar emerged from his throat. Behind him, Ardenhead's mouth was flooded with liquid silver, and current poured out, madbrain, blinding—

The bolt missed the man, but it blasted through Ingishead's cheek, leaving a gaping hole. Drumfire came from the smoking mask, and a sucking sound. As Arden watched, the side of Ingishead's face collapsed. Fountains of hail and the blink of broken circuits appeared through the hole.

Ingis seemed not to notice. Combs of current grew from his arms. Ingishead was still brimming with juice. A fresh bolt battered Ardenhead's chin. Another struck the beam of its nose. Ardenhead lurched. And then a second strike hit Arden, this one more powerful than the first.

He felt it before it landed. Electric shells enclosed him, one snug, one looser, one looser still, like you'd add wool and leather when the weather was cold. The shells all pressed at once, squeezing him, and a glowing wire fell on his brow like a hammer blow.

Arden sank to his knees.

Was the sky convulsing, or was it him? Through a dream haze, he saw Ingishead's beak open, and a silver-blue bolt shot out. It crashed through Ardenhead's temple, shattering its crown, and a load of hail came down, bombarding the Balcony.

Arden tried to stand. Over Ardenhead's crumpled cheek, gouts of vapor poured from the wound. The great temple was stove-in, his left eye collapsed— Through the gash, Arden could see the inside of his Vault, a span of its coffered ceiling.

Estra was shouting, crying out. What was she saying?

The hail stopped. The cranes were shrieking. He tried to stand, but— His body was shaking. Beneath him the Balcony swirled and recongealed.

Estra was beside him now, stooping over him. He could see lightning glance off her hair and chin. Ingishead's Cranium was crackling, brewing more juice. The electric claws were sharpening. Was it his fate, Arden thought, to be consumed?

She was speaking, but he couldn't hear her over the

thunder. Did he answer her? No, he was cramped and grunting. She clutched his middle. The fresh charge was mounting. Estra was shouting. The Balcony chattered with bullet rain.

Pain poured out of him— What was he saying? Maybe Estra knew.

She grabbed him and pulled him toward the Mouth.

Ingis struck again, and the blast ripped gobbets out of the opening. But that didn't stop her. Estra dragged him off the Balcony, into the Salon.

10

The oval room was tipping like a shipwreck. Jolts had overturned the bed, and the floor was sliding through the Mouth like an outgoing tide.

"Arden—"

Estra had her arm around his middle. She was helping him to stand.

He straightened, feeling his chest swimming over his legs. "I'm fine," he said, feeling the judders subside. "Fine." He blinked, turning his head.

"Are you sure?"

He didn't answer. His heart teetered between fright and dismay.

Another bolt from Ingis struck high, and the ceiling shook. Arden swung around, facing the Mouth. "I have to—" A flash dazzled him, and then Ingishead boomed.

"Dribbling brains, tangy bowels," Ingis bellowed from his Eyehole.

Estra was silent, motionless.

"Come out here," Ingis demanded.

"I'm not giving up," Arden said.

Estra shook her head. "You can't fight him the way you are."

A deafening *crack*, and the rear wall of the Salon opened like a giant clam. Wind stormed through the opening, hurling Arden and Estra through the slumped archway, into the Vault.

Estra gathered herself, rising, helping Arden up, holding him close to steady him. Together they scanned the ceiling. The blows from Ingis had torn out two spans and the portion of dome they supported. On either side, the canopy was collapsing. Icicles fell, along with filagreed hoar. Around the gash, dark shreds of vapor hung, drizzling.

"We still have power," Arden said.

The center of the Vault was still roiling, loaded with clashing hail, sparks and electric thorns.

Estra's expression was doubtful. "I'm not sure it will hold."

Cupolas were sagging at every angle. The walls lower down were scalloped and peeling, and the pillars were twisting.

A warbling howl pierced the air, rattling them both.

Fog—a large sheet—drifted over their heads. An inverted triangle. A wet tail hung from it, dark and raveling, and as it passed, it slid over Arden's back.

"The man on the cloud." Estra followed the scrap of fog with her eyes.

The derelict soul howled again, louder this time, descending the scale.

Arden shuddered. Its arms were spread wide— It was searching, headless; or embracing an endless anguish. The murdered man's soul passed over them again, and a gray devil rose from the floor, twisting Estra's hair.

Ingishead thundered, and Arden felt the trembling in every mote, as if his life with Estra was a dream on the verge of dissolving. The triangle soul flew beneath a cloister, and hung itself there like an empty coat.

"I'll Nurse My Rage back," he said, looking at Estra.

Dark thoughts, a breathless silence— Estra watched him.

He followed the Practice, opening wounds from his past. A few were gone, but most were still there. He imagined Mariod at his side, releasing his hand. He was flogged, piked. Alone at the Rink. Shuddering with juice. Ardenhead's charge was spiking, crackling above him. Shame, rage— Shame and fear—

Estra's eyes were pitying, tragic.

I'm weak, Arden thought—that's what she sees. Damaged. Sinking. Bogged in despair.

Wind whistled through the gash in the Vault. He heard the tinkle and clatter of falling ice. The crackling from Ingishead mounted.

Arden fixed on Estra. "I'll fight to the death with every volt I have left."

She bowed her head.

A bolt tore through the Vault lower down, dissolving a tier of cloisters, fog shrapnel flying in every direction.

"He doesn't care if he hits you," Arden said.

Her face crumpled. "Forgive me."

For what? What was she thinking?

Estra met his gaze, her eyes streaming. "That beautiful face—" She touched his brow. "I was the one who disfigured you."

Another bolt struck the Vault's ceiling, exploding ribs and the crowns between.

"The Arden I loved," Estra said, "I've turned over to him."

She spoke as if he was already gone.

"We're puppets," she said.

"I'm not giving up—"

A giant sickle, silver-blue, cut through the floor, quaking the Vault, dividing it in two. Arden and Estra clung to each other.

She groaned as the bolt withdrew. "Look what he's doing," she sobbed at the ragged hole in the floor.

"Why?" she shrieked, scrabbling the air around her head.

Arden stared at her, trying to understand.

"Look at him!" She raised her face, eyeing Ingishead's billows, visible now through the gaping ceiling. "Look, look! Can we fight?" she shrieked. "Can we leave?" Her voice echoed in the Vault. "Where? Where can we go?"

She shook her head at Arden. "Everything I do— Everything! Where I sleep, misery enters."

Arden's lips parted. He had to say something, but he didn't know what.

"I made a hell of heaven," she said. "Twice."

"You're thinking of leaving me."

"No—"

"You're going back to him."

She closed her eyes, and her voice grew soft. "I won't let him devour you. I love you—too much."

"Estra," Arden pleaded. "Don't do this to me."

A dozen cranes flew through the breach in the ceiling, stuttering as they descended, wheeling around them. Claps shook Ardenhead from below, Ingis striking its neck like a toiler swinging an ax at a tree.

"This is my fate," Estra said. "To do this for you. Find a cloud at the other end of the sky. Or return through a Tunnel. Go back to being the man I met in the forest."

"A toiler. A slave."

"Be kind," Estra said. "It's our last moment together."

"You were born for the biggest storm." His words dripped with acid. "I was just along for the ride. I know you, Estra."

She shook her head. "You don't know."

She kissed him, smiled through her tears and kissed him again. Then she huffed and hugged him with both arms, forcing their motes together one last time.

"Goodbye," she whispered.

Arden locked his arms around her and squeezed. Her middle compressed, and her chest spilled over his arms, like steam over a boiling pot's rim.

"What are you doing? Let me go—"

He clasped her tighter. She gasped, but she couldn't speak.

The outer cloisters were gone. The archway leading into the Salon had collapsed. Arden dragged her through the misty wreckage. He was boiling now, while Ardenhead shook around him. Ingis was still hacking at its neck.

It was all for Ingis, Arden thought. Her quivering lips, her moony looks, her scattered air— She acted repelled. Oh, she'd had enough. But when Ingis appeared, she couldn't resist. His power, his juice— It was as simple as that.

She'd never known or cared who he was, Arden thought. At the Pond, she was whispering to Ingis. When they Practiced, she was conjuring Ingis. In Estra's eyes, there was only one storm. He could blast Ingis out of his Eyehole and eat him alive— It wouldn't make any difference.

Love. Arden shuddered. He'd imagined it all. Not an honest word had ever passed Estra's lips.

"No," she cried. "No—" Estra's eyes grew wide.

He planted himself beside the Vat and lifted her.

"Ingis, Ingis," Arden seethed. "Think about Ingis."

He hurled her over the rim. Estra's head and shoulders plunged through the windings. The moment the gyre had hold of her, her protests ended.

"I'm washing him out of you," Arden said. "For good."

The remains of the Salon shimmied around him, and the fierce claps stopped. Had Ingis severed Ardenhead's neck? Arden gripped the Vat's rim. "Think about Ingis," he bellowed at Estra.

220

Cranes flew through the Mouth, stuttering, distressed, swooping around him, backflapping over the Vat, wings crinkling like the cast skins of snakes.

Estra sank and resurfaced. She slid onto her back, limp, eyes glazed.

"Going back to Ingis?" he said. "You won't remember his name."

The count, he thought. It was six the last time.

The black and gray gyre was corded at the rim, twisted tightly at its center. Estra rolled as he watched, turning facedown.

One, two, three—

A deafening *rip*, and a roar from the Vault, as if what remained of its ceiling had all at once given way. Arden heard it, but his gaze didn't waver. He could see the dark solvent washing through Estra. Four, five, six, seven— He drew a deep breath. He'd never used the Vat on his own.

The cranes settled. Eight, nine, ten— While he counted, they paced and squabbled.

Eleven, twelve, thirteen— Was he counting too fast? No chance of that. There was plenty of Ingis in her. Was she thinking about him?

"I want us to be together," Arden told her.

Another *rip*, Ardenhead tipped and righted.

"It's over for you," he shouted at Ingis. "Eight, nine, ten," he resumed, counting out loud, reassured by the sound of his voice. He remembered: the night on the ghost ship, when Estra left him; the moment in the Hanging Garden, when she explained. They had washed themselves in the Vat, but the cleansing hadn't been deep enough.

"A few seconds more," he said. "Just a few."

A bolt struck Ardenhead's face, jolting the wrecked Salon, dashing fog over the Vat's rim. Through the mangled Mouth, Arden could see pieces of the giant nose floating free. What was the count?

From the Vat's surface, a screech rose—like a strangling gull—a nightmare sound, mindless, inhuman. Estra sank beneath the whirling furrows.

It was as if a wind from the pole had struck him. Had she been in the Vat too long? Arden bent over the rim. He couldn't see through the corded surface. Was she turning just beneath?

He plunged his arm in and touched something—her back, her leg? The dark whorls gleamed, the center sucked with intent. He hung on to the rim with one hand and swept his arm through the windings. Nothing.

What have I done? he thought.

The cranes gabbled, Ingis continued to roar. Arden was trembling. He had to retrieve her. But— How could he go in and get out by himself?

He put his hand on his chest, then he pushed his finger inside it, searching the space over his heart. He found the linty end and pulled, drawing the wishing line under his chin, collecting loops of slack. He tied its end to a crusty knob on the Vat's side.

Then he curled over the rim, immersing himself.

He felt instantly groggy—unbothered, pacific. But his care for Estra, and his fear for her, overcame his torpor. He wrenched himself double and headed down. The ichor was thick. His movements were slow, dreamlike; and it was perfectly silent. There was enough light from above that he could see a half-dozen feet ahead.

A long shape in the solvent— Long and dark, flexed in the middle. He reached out, but his hands passed through. The shadow of an islet of foam on the surface. The wishing line brought him up short. He pulled on it, giving himself more slack, diving deeper.

The walls of the Vat were funnel-shaped, and he had to fight the whirling. He circled the walls, down and down. It grew dimmer. His legs slowed, and so did his arms. Where was he? Why was he here?

Estra, he thought. Then he cleared his mind, so he wouldn't erase her.

A few furious strokes, and he reached the bottom. There was nothing in sight.

Arden turned, feeling the walls where the funnel converged, waving his hands through the solvent. No body, no shreds— Nothing.

The Vat was empty. Estra was gone.

A few moments later, he was back on the surface, wondering how he had gotten there and why he was pulling himself up the wishing line. He stared at the Vat as the gyres went round, trying to grasp what had happened. He'd put Estra in, but something had gone wrong.

Arden turned. The ruined room swiveled around him. He was like a mouse on a potter's wheel. The cranes stood, tilting as one, all silent, all staring. Ardenhead, he thought. The cloud was ravaged. The Mouth swirled with fog. The upper lip was missing and the threshold was swamped.

He reeled toward it. Ingis, he thought.

Through the opening, he could see the monstrous boils, thick as a stew. Ingis was stirring it with a crusty spoon, and with every *crunch*, his charge lit the darkness.

Arden felt gutted. Was his heart gone? He struggled to accept what had happened. A man, ruling the skies from his own floating head, and a woman who lived there with him— None of it seemed real. It was the dream of someone who was dying, the last glimpse of a life left behind.

He crossed the threshold and stepped out onto the Balcony.

Ingishead filled his sight—boils on boils, its blasted cheek seeping, its thunder shaking the air. Black rashers hung from its neck, pouring torrents. And below that, Arden saw water—a thousand black lozenges, each with a collar of foam. When he looked up, Ingis was there.

The Eyehole flashed like a silver iris, and the man stood perfectly centered, like the pupil of a cat.

"You're fog," Arden said. "You belong to the void."

Ingis didn't reply. He looked puzzled, uncertain. He gazed at the Mouth, waiting for Estra to appear. In a rush, the cranes streamed through it, mobbing the space between the two giant heads, shrieking, flapping, wind checkering their backs, crushing their wings, making snakes of their necks.

Ingis listened as the birds' cries turned into a dirge, following their panic with what looked like suspicion.

"Where is Estra?" He stared at Arden.

Ardenhead heaved, its bashed face awash, brow half dissolved, crown gone. Arden's hands were numb from the Vat, his feet, his legs— He shook his head.

"Where is she?" Ingis demanded.

"She's not coming back." Arden's voice quavered.

Ingis was mute, disbelieving. His thunder faded.

"You crazy fool," Ingis said in the hush.

Then Arden saw his contempt rising. How dare you, Ingis' eyes said. As if, despite all that had happened, Arden had no claim on his queen. Then his contempt turned into disgust. How had such a lowly creature wormed his way into heaven?

Ingishead strobed. An electric field was spreading. Arden felt himself buzzing, like a fly in a web, caught, shaken. He could see Ingishead's energy mounting—the livid boils, the wiry leaders, the tufts and jags— The great head was straining, unable to contain itself.

A sword shot out, striking a few feet away, blasting to bits the right side of the Balcony. The cheek above steamed and smoked. Ingishead's features transformed, creased by fissures, swollen by boils—appalled, murderous, grieving, hateful—

Amid Arden's guilt and gloom, indignation rose. From Mariod, from Estra, from his beggary and subjection—his rage bloomed. It didn't need to be nursed.

Ardenhead was in ruins, its face gouged, the great Vault

blasted— But charges still flickered within, and there were wires at his call. He strung them through the swimming rubble with hardly a thought, shooting them in the direction of Ingis, one after another. One struck low of the Eyehole, two missed completely, another passed through Ingishead's neck, fraying in the sky at its rear.

Ingishead roared and returned a bolt, barely missing, burning a hole over Arden's shoulder.

The mob of cranes grew. Birds from both storms were screeching and wheeling in the space between them. Arden paid no mind. He was lost in his fury, hurling currents like a toiler in a brawl, swinging wild, so eaten by anguish that he didn't care. A lucky wire nicked the Eyehole's rim. Another striped Ingishead's nose.

Ingis was not so unbridled. He let a billow loose from his crown and blew it over Ardenhead, dumping a torrent. Water flowed down the riddled face, and Arden was drenched and grounded. A lightning scythe pierced the tattered lip, and current descended, passing through him. Flash—

Blindness consumed him. Arden shook, then his sight came back.

Another strike. Flash—the black convulsions again.

And another. Flash, then black. Arden shook and shook, wondering if his sight would return. When it did, all he could see was the Cranium looming, and all he could hear was its deafening roar. He was alone now, a failing man on a ruined cloud.

"I'm the fool," he raised his fists at Ingis. "Strike me!"

My last words, Arden thought. A deep rumble was mounting—he could feel it in every mote. A fierce charge—mind-stopping fear, uncontrollable shaking—

"Strike me," he screamed.

A giant sword unsheathed, razor-edged and molten bright. It flashed toward the Balcony, striking beneath, driving up into the demolished Salon. Gloating explosions, thundering wrath— Ingis was thrusting, following the stroke again and again.

The Balcony heaved beneath him. Flung high, barely whole—

Arden was like a star, spread-eagled, turning through space. Were his limbs being ripped from his frame? Turning, turning, lost in the night; but still he heard the roar and the screaming. Was it his jaw that gaped, his voice that echoed in the sightless void?

He slowed—buoyed, weightless—fighting to hold on to his thoughts. He was intact. Still alive. But electric convulsions were clamping the sky around him. In the distance, a tiny moon sank in an ocean of fog. Before him—

The billows of the Cranium churned. A stray wind circled and sucked him among them, and he entered the monstrous head. On either side, vapors coiled, weaving and knotting like giant eels, breeding or eating each other, bloated entrails, purple and black—

The thick boils engulfed him. The storm's damp filled his lungs. He was gagging, choking— Do you belong to Ingis? he thought. Will you give all you have left, to him?

Through a gap in the billows, he could see the boudoir. Ingis was turning away from the Eyehole. He stepped toward the oversized bed, folding his arms, staring at the place where Estra had slept. Grieving her. Unaware he was being watched.

Arden's hatred was deep. The vapors around him were caustic, burning him, shrinking him, liquescing his motes— Was there any charge left in Ardenhead? Could he draw a bolt from where he was? He focused, reaching back into the Vault, feeling for a spark, a thorn, a kink of juice. The giant self still had power.

"More?" Arden raged. "I'll give you more." He fixed on Ingis.

The man looked up.

Arden drew out his current—all of it, everything he had. The sky shook with thunder— A great clap and a megavolt charge— The air in the boudoir turned to fire, and the blinding bolt blasted Arden up, through Ingishead's crown.

As his sight came back, he saw the Cranium open. A stroke through the Eyehole had sliced it in two. Its top half was lifting like a cracked skull. Arden spread his arms and legs. He was a star again, floating in space.

The blasted skull was a chaos of fountaining hail and crossed swords, whirling soot and vipering scarves— The roar was deafening. The cranes of Ingis were circling the detaching crown. Then another flock took wing. Free at last, howling in unison, the souls Ingis had taken rushed from the gap, triangles spread, flying in every direction.

The Cranium's crown floated free, rocking in a night thick with stars. Its glittering coffers and icicle hives sparked and arced. The lancets pinched, and the boils deflated. Then its charge jittered, and the crown went dark.

Arden searched the skull's base. Ingis was splayed across the oversized bed in the steaming boudoir. He tried to raise himself and sank back down.

Arden fixed on the motionless man. He tried to string a wire—a doubtful puppeteer, hoping for one last tug. The energy was there, and the charge was larger than he expected. Before it struck, the base of Ingishead glowed and sparked. Then it exploded, splashing the night with tatters and puffs.

The cranes of Ingis wove through the drifting mass, their stutter like a dying prayer. The giant neck fell like a dead snake, tangling as it reached the shoreline below. Slowly the stutters faded, and the stranded cranes became scarves of mist.

"Look what we did," Arden said, thinking of Estra.

Then he pushed the thoughts away.

He faced Ardenhead, crossed his wrists over his chest, bent his knees, and threw himself forward. The winds were streaming, but he tumbled through them, spreading his arms as he approached, straightening his legs to descend.

He landed on the remains of the Balcony, and from there he steered Ardenhead through the drifting shreds. Most of his neck was gone, but the winds around the stump were lively, and they swirled as he moved, sweeping up the vestiges. There were sparks and thorns in every one, and as the stray pieces passed into his Throat, Arden heard the crackling and felt the friction.

That infirm feeling, the sense of weakness in so many parts— It won't last long, he thought. The first of Ingishead's digested remains were rising into the damaged Vault.

With every hour that passed, his thunderhead healed. Arden fed deliberately, sucking up shreds without gorging. The fresh vapors billowed inside him, and the charge in the Vault grew and grew.

Night was ending, and the stars were falling. No, the stars were still; it was Ardenhead that was rising, gaining thousands of feet. He scanned the field, still littered with pieces of Ingishead.

From behind a large puff, a gray raft appeared.

The oversized bed from Estra's boudoir.

On it was a huddled shape—like a man. A body with limbs and a head.

As Arden drove his storm closer, his winds stretched the bed and pulled the man off it. One leg was bent at an odd angle. His arms seemed disconnected as well. Then the head turned.

Ingis hung in the air before him, unable to move, looking defiant.

How many had stories like theirs, Arden thought. People who escaped to the sky with high hopes, lived a short life there and disappeared.

"You don't have much time," Arden said.

Ingis was blithe. "It's not time we seek in eternity. It's growth."

"Lofty ideas," Arden said. "You and Estra were alike in that."

Ingis peered at him. "What did she ever see in you? You didn't understand her."

Arden's winds swept Ingis up, and the Throat swallowed him whole.

Arden slept on the Balcony that night. He dreamt of Estra.

She stood at the Prow of the ghost ship, naked, silhouetted against an emerald sky. Her eyes were hidden and so was her face. The last blood of the sun was flowing into the sea, and in the cove of her flexed arm, a star was blinking. As he approached, she shivered and drew against him.

By morning, fresh billows had remade the Salon. The bed was a different shape, in a different place, and the Vat was gone. Maybe there was a new one, somewhere else.

Arden crossed the room. As he passed through the archway, he heard a duo of warbling howls. The soul of Ingis and the man taken from his cloud were howling together. Arden stepped into the Vault. An inverted triangle was gliding through the cloisters. Another was banging against an icy window. There was no sign of Estra. No soul. No sound. Not a whisper.

It was more than a Vault now. It was a Sanctum. Massive pillars—tubes of fog, twisted together—had raised the ceiling by thousands of feet. It shimmered with iridescent tiles and ropy moldings; droops of ice hung from every angle; and between the ribs, fretworks of frost and perforated screens lit the space. Giant eddies in the Sanctum's center crackled and sputtered, choked with juice.

The life of a cloud— Just air and water, motes and wind.

He remembered their first morning in the sky together. The cranes they'd created were circling the Sanctum, stuttering as they rode the warm currents of dawn. The birds and the memories squeezed his heart.

"Estra," he mumbled, begging her forgiveness. His eyes flooded, remembering their second day at the Pond. "We never found our harbor."

Ingis was right. Estra had been a mystery to him, and she always would be. Like a creature in a storybook Mariod read him, about an uncharted sea with a gorgon that lived in a hole beneath it.

For a moment, he imagined Estra was standing beside him, whispering in his ear like she had at the Pond. He raised his finger to write on the air. Then he turned to the blank skirt below the Sanctum's ceiling and traced her words. They appeared, incised in the fog, tall as a man: "King of Heaven, Beholden to None."

Rich Shapero's stories strike flashes of insight into realms unseen. His previous titles, *Rin, Tongue and Dorner, Arms from the Sea, The Hope We Seek, Too Far* and *Wild Animus*, combine book, music and visual art and are also available as multimedia tablet apps and ebooks. *The Village Voice* hailed his story experiences as "A delirious fusion of fiction, music and art," and Howard Frank Mosher called him a "spellbinding storyteller." He is the winner of a Digital Book World award for best adult fiction app. He lives with his wife and daughters in the Santa Cruz Mountains.